The One-Handed Pianist and Other Stories

Also by Ilan Stavans

Fiction

The Disappearance

Nonfiction

The Hispanic Condition
Art and Anger
The Riddle of Cantinflas
Imagining Columbus
The Inveterate Dreamer
Octavio Paz: A Meditation
Bandido
On Borrowed Words
Spanglish
¡Lotería! (with Teresa Villegas)
Dictionary Days
Love and Language (with Verónica Albin)

Anthologies

Growing Up Latino (with Harold Augenbraum)
Tropical Synagogues
The Oxford Book of Latin American Essays
The Oxford Book of Jewish Stories
Mutual Impressions
Wáchale!
The Scroll and the Cross
The Schocken Book of Modern Sephardic Literature
Lengua Fresca (with Harold Augenbraum)

Cartoons

Latino USA (with Lalo Alcaraz)

Translations

Sentimental Songs by Felipe Alfau

Editions

The Collected Stories by Calvert Casey
The Poetry of Pablo Neruda
Collected Stories by Isaac Bashevis Singer (three volumes)
Encyclopedia Latina (four volumes)
Selected Writings by Rubén Darío
I Explain a Few Things by Pablo Neruda
An Organizer's Tale by César Chávez

General

The Essential Ilan Stavans
Ilan Stavans: Eight Conversations (with Neal Sokol)
Conversations with Ilan Stavans
Collins Q&A: Latino History and Culture

Ilan Stavans

The One-Handed Pianist

AND OTHER STORIES

Northwestern

University Press

Evanston, Illinois

These stories first appeared in Spanish in two volumes: *Talia y el cielo* (1979; rev. 1989) and *La pianista manca* (1992). Translations were sponsored by a generous grant from the Lucius N. Littauer Foundation. "A Heaven Without Crows" was first published in English in *Michigan Quarterly Review* and *Cross Currents;* "The Invention of Memory" in *Alaska Quarterly Review;* "The Death of Yankos" in *Calypso* and *Tropical Synagogues: Short Stories by Jewish-Latin American Writers* (Holmes & Meier, 1994) ; "The One-Handed Pianist" in *TriQuarterly;* segments of "Talia in Heaven" in *Southwest Review* and *The Literary Review;* "The Spot" in *Confrontations;* "House Repossessed" in *Massachusetts Review* and *Under the Pomegranate Tree,* Ray Gonzalez, ed. (Pocket Books, 1996); "Three Nightmares" in *The Literary Review;* and "Lost in Translation" in *Massachusetts Review* and *Currents from the Dancing River,* Ray Gonzalez, ed. (Harcourt Brace, 1994).

Translated by Dick Gerdes, Harry Morales, Amy Prince, Alison Stavchansky, David Unger, and the author.

Northwestern University Press
www.nupress.northwestern.edu

Northwestern University Press edition published 2007. Copyright © 1996 by Ilan Stavans.
First published 1996 by the University of New Mexico Press. All rights reserved.

Printed in the United States of America

10   9   8   7   6   5   4   3   2   1

Library of Congress Cataloging-in-Publication Data
Stavans, Ilan.
    [Short stories. English. Selections]
    The one-handed pianist and other stories / Ilan Stavans.—Northwestern University Press ed.
    p. cm.
    Previously published: Albuquerque : University of New Mexico Press, 1996.
    ISBN-13: 978-0-8101-2460-8 (pbk. : alk. paper)
    ISBN-10: 0-8101-2460-2 (pbk. : alk. paper)
    1. Stavans, Ilan—Translations into English. I. Title.
PQ7079.2.S78A27 2007
  863.64—dc22

                          2007017827

∞ The paper used in this publication meets the minimum requirements of the American National Standard for Information Sciences—Permanence of Paper for Printed Library Materials, ANSI Z39.48-1992.

Designed by Linda Mae Tratechaud

EGOTIST, n.
A person of low taste,
more interested in himself
than in me.
　　　—AMBROSE BIERCE, *THE DEVIL'S DICTIONARY*

Contents

THE ONE-HANDED PIANIST AND OTHER STORIES

A HEAVEN WITHOUT CROWS

21, V, 1924
Kierling Sanatorium
Klosterneuberg

DEAR MAX,[*]

THANKS FOR HAVING COME TEN DAYS AGO TO VISIT THIS OLD INVALID WHO'S about to say goodbye. Just a few miles from Vienna and already I feel I'm in the Other World. I have tuberculosis in the larynx, I know, though the doctors persist in offering other diagnoses, incredible beyond belief. Why won't anyone dare to talk honestly to a dying man? Death is the issue and still they're vague, evasive. Dr. Tschiassny tells me that my throat is looking much better but I don't believe him; I can't even swallow solid food any more, so I live on lemonade, beer, wine, and water. They apply ice packs to my throat on a regular basis. I've also been given medicated lozenges and Demropon which, till now, has been ineffective in treating my cough.

---

[*] I feel great anguish when I consider Franz Kafka's request that his friend Max Brod burn his writings. What could have motivated the writer to insist that his artistic production be destroyed? Perhaps his profound antinomic nature, though that only seems to me half the truth. I have searched in vain through the back alleys of his writings, as well as by reading biographies. I offer, therefore, my own explanation, at once sensible and farfetched, contained in this letter never sent to Brod, composed two weeks before the Czech writer died.

I

I admit that if it weren't for Dr. Klopstock from Budapest—"the madman," as you refer to him—who I met that frigid February in 1921, I wouldn't even be writing to you now. He takes good care of me, though at times I suspect he's at bottom a hypocrite. He has promised to inject me with sedatives when the pain becomes unbearable; we'll see what happens. Yes, I know there's a vial of camphor ready for me in the medicine chest. Dora Diamant, my dear Dora, trusts him implicitly and that pleases me. They take turns sitting at my side when I can't stay alone. I'm extremely grateful, though I tell them there's no reason to prolong the agony. Guess what? Yesterday late at night an owl perched right outside my window. The bird of death!

You've seen me: 103 pounds fully dressed. I've lost my voice and can only be heard if I whisper—which isn't so bad coming from me. They've suggested that Dora end my treatment and take me home, but she refuses. I'm completely in favor! Dying in a hospital is too impersonal. Furthermore, all this is very expensive—as if one has to pay taxes to a sultan before checking out. Soon I'll get some money from Otto Pick and Prager Presse for the "Josephine" story; also, Die Schmiede owes me a check. If they're sent to you, pass them on to Dora to pay the bills.

When you visited me, we could barely communicate. You claim I was too absorbed, as if hiding a secret, and that my gestures were strange. We talked about my October 22, 1922 request, in which I expressed my final wishes regarding my writings. Since you could make yourself understood and I couldn't I would like to clarify again what I meant: I'll also mention an astonishing and sad development which, I'm afraid, will perhaps disturb our friendship. On the same day of your visit I got the unpleasant news that Dora's father, after consulting with a rabbi, had rejected our wish to marry. But that's another story.

Of all my writings, you know that the only ones of value are *The Trial*, "The Stoker," "The Metamorphosis," "In the Penal Colony," "A Country

Doctor," and "A Hunger Artist." (You can save the few remaining copies of *Meditations* since I don't want to give anyone the work of eliminating them— still, none of its stories can be reprinted.) When I say these writings have value, I don't mean to imply they should be reprinted or saved for posterity; on the contrary, my deepest wish would be for them to disappear completely from sight. But everything else in newspapers, magazines, papers, manuscripts, letters—barring nothing—, should be retrieved from the people who have them and burned, preferably without being read. I can't stop you from reading them, but I wouldn't like it; in no way should anyone other than you set eyes upon them.

You asked me: why destroy writings that are already part of humanity? I apologize for not having known how to answer. At first I thought of telling you it was an impulse, an inexplicable premonition. But I understand what you are saying: what is art if not an attempt to transcend death? Isn't art the trace which remains when we are no longer on this earth? That's why I thought of saying that nothing imperfect should survive and what I've written is imperfect, even though I have spent many nights wide awake changing a defective phrase here or there or looking for the right touch of humor. That which is imperfect causes in me great embarrassment. Many times we've discussed Flaubert and his "irritating"—this is your word, dear friend— meticulousness. Doesn't he state in his letters to Turgenev and to his dearly beloved Louise Colet that he spent months, even years, looking for the ideal word, revising a single page over and over? And what is the right word? No one knows. Or better: only God knows.

Now more than ever I understand my hesitancy regarding my Jewish heritage. I yearn for the immemorial time when a library consisted of just the Whole Book, the one that transcribes Suffering, Truth, and the Law. My father Herrmann is true to his religion though he partakes of its rituals mechanically and without question. His severe, authoritarian manner instills terror. It's difficult for me to get close to him and I suppose K.'s indecision and incapacity in *The Castle* is inspired by him. My idea of God is of a distant warden in a state of alertness, always ready to punish. Is this the same God who wrote the Book of Books? If so, he must've written it in a burst of rage, taking pleasure in the dreadfulness of his creations.

Now I feel I've mocked my father. Fresh in my mind is the letter I wrote him when you and I were in Schelesin. Remember? I had to tell him about my endless yearning for childhood and the suffering I endured under his implacable yoke. I'm sure the death of the two babies my mother bore after I was born was traumatic; truth is they, not I, deserved to live. I have a clear memory in mind: I was a young boy and, on a night like so many others, I was whining, begging for water. It wasn't only that I was thirsty, I also wanted to enjoy myself. Suddenly my father came in, dragged me out of bed and took me to the balcony. He left me there locked up till I grew calm. That was his style—intolerant and demanding. The event left me scarred. From that day on, I dream about a huge man, a judge who comes to pull me out of my bedroom and condemns me. What I leave behind in my writings is a variation on that dream—a handful of complaints which lack the least bit of interest—, the view of a conflicted person. Is there any hope in a kingdom where cats chase after a mouse? Yes, but not for the mouse.

For many years this has been my view: nevertheless, today I feel its hypocrisy and inconsistency. My father always wanted to see me as a successful son, which makes me wonder: Does God perceive us as we are? I'm sure he does. Any other way, then, would be our fault. The weakened and tense relationship with my father is more my fault than his. I take pleasure in playing the role of Jesus Christ—the martyr who suffers for others. Deep down I am an actor specializing in submissive characters. An actor who knows how to create something out of his own being. Is my father truly so severe and authoritarian? Perhaps. Valli, Ottla, and Elli (the latter to a lesser extent) also complain about his character, though they have the benefit of being females. To a larger degree, my father is just like my uncles Philip, Heinrich, and Ludwig, at times even more sensitive than they. Tell me then why aren't any of my cousins—Otto, Oskar, Victor, and the others—afraid? Because I am an impostor who has invented a dark reality. Because I've made a career out of being a victim.

How embarrassing for me to reveal to you at age forty-one my hateful comedy. Did you suspect it already? Of course. Why haven't I burned my own writings? The answer is not cowardice but rather because I'm a person weakened by vanity. Deep inside I know very well you too won't set them ablaze; on the contrary, they're useful to you since your own novels fill you with uncertainty. To achieve a kind of immortality, my books would depend on my own immolation, on creating a legend; one would have to read them in the light of all the errors of a poor crucified Jew who detested himself so much. Is there a more fascinating creature than the one who first describes a detestable world and then censures himself?

Now I'm getting to the heart of this letter. Years ago, during the time when I forced myself to learn Hebrew, I met in Studl's boarding house Julie Wohryzek, a beautiful, if a bit foolish, girl. You know the story very well—I've recounted it to you many times, but not its outcome. Her father was a cobbler who also carried out a few administrative tasks in the synagogue. She was neither Jew nor gentile, German nor otherwise. She had a light-hearted spirit; every time we were together, she was laughing. She had been engaged, but her fiancé died in the war. Julie reminded me of Grete Bloch, the woman with whom I had an unhappy romance unbeknownst to my fiancée Felice. I felt both desire and anxiety with Julie.

Winter brought us together in an old-fashioned room that smelled of ammonia. We were there for a month and a half. Our intimacy, with its implied sexuality, frightened me. Julie did not want to get married and from the start she denied any interest in procreation. We were both happy with the relationship; nevertheless, I saw her change in this respect, till she began to yearn for children: she said that being pregnant is "a privilege no woman should renounce." Our first separation was in March of 1919. We reunited in April in Prague and our intimacy grew even more intense. We became engaged and rented an apartment in Wrschowitz. My parents, of course, were against this. Around this time we received copies of "The Penal Colony" from Kurt Wolff Verlag. I remember how with enthusiasm I gave my father one copy. As soon as he saw it, he snuffed my happiness and said with scorn "Put it on my desk!" I felt humiliated. A little later, when I announced in the living room our betrothal, they created a scene. My father insinuated that Julie was a common Prague girl—you could tell by her dress and her manners—and my mother agreed without saying a word. All this filled me with doubt, and days later we lost our lease. I decided then to break this— my third—engagement. We separated; Julie, who was twenty-eight years old, was deeply hurt and moved to another city. We separated for a second time, promising to continue writing to each other but didn't. I never heard from her again.

Till a few weeks ago, when I received an airmail letter mailed to my parents' home with no return address. She gave me the astonishing news that my son Zdenek Saul Kafka Wohryzek was four years old. She told me he's a chubby boy with brown eyes and he lost his first tooth in November. He has a scar on his chin from when he tripped in school, hitting his head against a sharp metal edge. His mother added that in a few weeks the two of them would be heading off to America. She didn't say a thing about a reconciliation.

Did this unsettle me? I gasped for breath and lost my balance. When no one was looking, I burnt the letter. Yes, burned it up. What else could I do? You know very well I could never be a father; to have children is to begin a journey toward redemption, and salvation is not for me but for my nullity. Since then I've tried unsuccessfully to put the incident behind me. Furthermore, I'm possessed by an old saying which I repeat day and night till I am worn out. Do you remember it? It's the one about all the crows boasting that just a single crow could destroy the heavens, which proves nothing since the heavens are nothing more than the negation of crows. I mentioned this to a German doctor who periodically reexamines me and he smiled, realizing that Kavka means "crow" in Czech.

Wait, there's more. There's a prostitute here among the sanatorium patients and I sit with her on the terraza to take some sun. She's a fortune-teller, and one day she wanted to read my future. She took hold of my right hand and opened it. When she saw the lines on my palm, she became suddenly silent, unable to hold back a cry of sorrow. She then assured me that though my own future was dark, my son was in good hands. My heart began to race. I told her I had no offspring but she explained that my son was in excellent health and soon would be arriving in New York. She added that the immigration authorities wouldn't let him enter and he—would sail throughout the Caribbean until he reached a port where they spoke Spanish named Veri Crucci or Bara Crutz. And what did his future hold? He would be a merchant. He would begin selling knives and would end up with a successful paint business with a number of stores. A businessman, like his grandfather Herrmann. The former prostitute also said that during his adolescence he would search for me. He would visit my grave in Prague and would reclaim from you, Max, the rights to my books, but that you would ignore him.

Do you know how I felt? Covered with muck, full of filth. (Exactly what I felt when I finished *The Trial*). Dora, to whom I'll never be married, spent the next night at my side. She'll tell you I slept poorly and it's true, I had an awful nightmare. I dreamt that someone was washing my corpse with a soft and oily soap; he wrapped it in a white shroud and chopped it in a thousand pieces with a butcher knife. After he placed the pieces in a hole, I saw you, my parents and brothers, and a policeman writing the following words in stone: Evil does not exist, you have crossed the threshold, everything is fine.

I have the feeling my whole life has been a lie. As if I tried for years to go through a door and not succeeded because the lock seemed impenetrable though it really wasn't.

I have a pain in my chest. . . . Will we see each other again? If Zdenek seeks you out, please open the door. Please tell him that I was an actor and executioner.

Franz

⌐────╕

Translated by David Unger

THE INVENTION OF MEMORY

For Ishai P.

"Healing," Pop would tell me, "is not a science, but the intuitive art of wooing Nature."
W. H. Auden, *The Art of Healing*

Death is always on the way, but the fact that you don't know when it will arrive seems to take away from the finiteness of life. It's that terrible precision that we hate so much. But because we don't know, we get to think of life as an inexhaustible well. Yet everything happens only a certain number of times, and a very small number, really. How many more times will you remember a certain afternoon of your childhood, some afternoon that's so deeply a part of your being that you can't even conceive of your life without it? Perhaps four or five times more. Perhaps not even that. How many more times will you watch the full moon rise? Perhaps twenty. And yet it all seems limitless.
Paul Bowles, *The Sheltering Sky*

One has to begin to lose memory, even small fragments of it, to realize that memory is what our entire life is made of. A life without memory wouldn't be life, just as an intelligence without means of expression wouldn't be intelligence. Our memory is our coherence, our reason, our action, our feeling. Without it we aren't anything.
Luis Buñuel, *My Last Sight*

9

NIGHT HAD FALLEN. I WAS HAVING A SNACK AND HEARD NOISES: A CARDBOARD box being dragged across the floor, the tapping of a hammer, the telegraphic conversation in distorted syllables of three, maybe four, people. I was overtaken by curiosity and peeked from behind the curtains. I saw a moving van outside and some workers carrying in a lamp, a typewriter, and seemingly hundreds of numbered boxes. Moving should be done during the day, I said to myself. I went down to the kitchen, put the kettle on, and fixed a cup of tea. Eager to spy once again, I went back upstairs with my cup and sat down in front of the window.

After a few moments, I was able to perceive his silhouette: he was tall and thin and had an overabundant and curiously wild-looking beard. He was wearing a turtleneck sweater and dark pants. His round head reminded me of an Italian baritone singer who had worked with Abel in a presentation of *Don Giovanni* or *The Marriage of Figaro*, I don't remember which, at the National Auditorium. I remembered that Mrs. Debeikis had tried to predict the man's profession. More than an academic, he must have been a writer or a diplomat, even though the latter didn't seem appropriate for someone who was going to live in a neighborhood so far from embassy row and the government offices. I watched attentively. The door to No. 91 was partially open. I turned to see that the old widow, Mrs. Debeikis, sporting a cane that now seemed to become even more flimsy and useless, had gone outside to welcome them. While it occurred to me to go out and join them, I decided against it because it had been a trying day—I was too tired to make the effort. It was for the best; after all, I had decided to keep my contacts with the new neighbor to a minimum. The trials and tribulations of the previous renters in No. 58 had drained me, above all, the Becerra family, of whom both Abel and I had grown fond and whose departure had affected me profoundly; it was as if I had seen in their departure the fleeting nature of life, a universe composed of intense longing, of evanescent bubbles that appear suddenly, disperse, and then pop.

Early that morning my neighbor, Mrs. Debeikis, rang the doorbell. She had come to tell me that, finally, she had managed to rent the house across the street, No. 58. She would have called but, ever since the doctor had recommended she get some exercise, she would go out whenever the sun was shining or when she felt energetic, ready to battle the forces of death.

As I got to the door, I saw her cane through the peephole and understood immediately that she had some news. After having tried repeatedly to rent the house for eight months, perhaps a year, without success, she would become depressed every time she talked about it. It was obvious things had changed now.

The rent—during our conversation, she kept mentioning the rent. The sum wasn't very much; one might say, in fact, it was ridiculous. Indeed, she brought up the amount several times, as if she couldn't believe it herself or as if she wanted to blame the hard times—they were dismal then, as they always are—that faced the nation and, of course, the world at large. Ever since Abel and I started renting No. 85 over seven years ago, I remember her believing that her three real estate properties in Copilco, our own neighborhood, would increase in value. Sooner or later, the buyers would fight over them, she would say. It wasn't true, of course. Just another one of those convenient falsehoods people convince themselves of.

Mrs. Debeikis had widowed at an early age. According to what she had once told me, her husband, an investment banker with a pitiful vision of the stock exchange, had left her only these minuscule properties, which at the time of his death, decades ago, were almost worthless. They had hardly gone up in value. Her husband had been suffering from a liver cancer that killed him in two years. She was drained from the entire agony, burdened with debts, and had a young daughter still living with her. Happily, she took care of things as only suffering mothers know how, educating her daughter, working in her sister's floral shop, and renting out Nos. 58 and 85. Today, her daughter is married, has a child and lives far away—in Connecticut.

Mrs. Debeikis's brother-in-law, who helped her take care of her properties, had recommended time and again that she sell everything. "Things won't improve," he would say. Only then she would have no headaches; she wouldn't always have to be arguing with those ignorant plumbers, swindling locksmiths, nasty repairmen, and careless painters. But she resisted. First, because she depended on the rental income in order to live (recently, a monthly check that her daughter would send her from a bank in New York would also contribute to her daily allowance). She was afraid to sell her properties, and not know how to save enough money to last her for a lifetime, even if she was already at a fairly advanced age. And, second, because Mrs. Debeikis would say: "If I have to pay to have the plumbing, the rotting ceilings, and the broken door hinges fixed in my house . . . what difference does it make to deal with the problems of Nos. 58 and 85 as well?" Truth is, at seventy-four years of age, the old lady was becoming ever more intolerant of the repairmen, irregular rent checks, and the behavior of the renters.

She had told me that she had placed ads to rent No. 58 in the classified section of several newspapers in Mexico City. A friend of her son-in-law in the United States had even put her in contact with a realtor on Wall Street; perhaps some foreigner would be interested in the house. The commission would probably be high but so long as the place got rented, it would be worth it. She didn't get any offers, however. Not until now, at least.

Architecturally speaking, house No. 58 is only slightly more attractive than the one Abel and I rent. Both consist of a story and a half, two bathrooms, three bedrooms (the master bedroom is upstairs), kitchen, living room, a garden in the back, and a garage behind the entryway. Both are about 300 square feet in size. Large windows face onto the street; if I want, therefore, I can spy on my neighbors and they can also spy on us. According to Mrs. Debeikis, both houses were built at the same time, in 1962, by a man of

German descent, a Mr. Elías Fischer or Eliyau Fickter (his signature, scratched on the exterior of both structures next to the porticos, has been all but erased with time and it's difficult to decipher it). But he must have been more inspired when he designed the house in front. Whoever compares the one on this side to No. 58 would conclude that, despite its poor condition, it displays a more modern aesthetic, the courage to experiment that was typical at the time, an audaciousness absent in the architecture of No. 85.

The entryway on this side has a small black iron gate that is now rusted, a victim of neglect. On each side of the house, the bricklayers built walls with irregular-sized bricks in such a way that there are symmetrical holes everywhere, through which pedestrians walking down the sidewalk could peek inside and vice versa. Originally, those walls were white, but each new renter has added more coats of paint of different colors in order to give the place a distinct personality, a feeling of newness. Some ten years ago, Mrs. Debeikis allowed one renter to add an additional floor on the roof. The renovation changed the appearance of the house. The new room isn't anything more than a laundry room—in No. 85 the washing machine is next to the storage room—and an exercise room with a small gym machine. But the last three renters used the area for other purposes; one renter even installed a bar.

More than likely, its quirky construction, its strange appearance, will turn off any future renters; but the house has been rented four times since Abel and I have been living across from it. First a dental student inhabited it. He was the son of a multi-millionaire from up north, Monterrey, if I'm not mistaken. He would leave every day at 8:00 in the morning and return at 10:00 in the evening. An easy-going, cordial guy. His principal defect was the drinking—and there was also the noise. Every two or three weeks he would organize such loud, wild parties that even the Romans would be envious. The uproar produced by these orgies held on the witches' Sabbath was shocking. One would get the impression that these parties took place in our own garage and, if such strident noise could be heard in No. 85, then surely Mrs. Debeikis would hear it right inside her own eardrums. At one of the parties, early in the morning, one of the party-goers, who was screaming like Tarzan, threw an empty bottle of tequila at our bedroom window and broke it. The police came, the host had to apologize to us, and, by noon the next day, his father, who was in Nuevo Laredo at the time, had already sent two workmen to fix the window. Nevertheless, Mrs. Debeikis, who had always esteemed our friendship, apologized to us and gave a serious talk to the student. Apparently, she couldn't evict him because the rent contract stipulated that eviction was possible only under certain conditions, two of them being assault and destruction. The incident was followed by some months of peace, but the bedlam soon began again. Despite his shyness, Abel, who was possessive of the serenity and repose he enjoyed during his three-and-a-half evening hours of practicing the violin (in the mornings the clamor of automobiles and trucks disturbed him), had to lodge a complaint. As a result, No. 58 was empty in a matter of weeks.

Then a family rented the house. Their name was Becerra. The mother, a German, spoke horrible Spanish. Her husband had been a politician and had worked in the Office of Tourism during the initial years of the José López Portillo regime. But there had been a scandal and he was sent to jail for corruption. The couple had moved to Cuernavaca and then to Copilco in Mexico City, intending to start over. He had bought a sausage factory in Tlalpan. They had two daughters, the youngest of which was mentally retarded. The older one, already an adolescent at the time, played ball and jacks on the patio while the other would look at her and laugh, benevolently, with that simplicity common to Down's syndrome people. Sometimes their friends would come to visit and they would spread out a bunch of dolls under the portico. I would greet them in the mornings, before heading off for classes. The older daughter would ask me if that day I was going to tell my students about Cuauthémoc or Hernán Cortés, two names she had learned at school. And Abel, who feels intimidated by children and, from the very day we got married made it absolutely clear that he was opposed to procreation because his musical career was the most important and it deserved all of his attention, would give them candy and gifts on Halloween; in time, he indeed became quite fond of them. I used to tell him that around the girls he seemed like a good-natured uncle, as he would always laugh around them. When he would return from a rehearsal or giving a concert at the university, the two girls would run to greet him, always ready to give him a kiss. Since their cousins lived far away in Berlin or Frankfurt, I forget which, he became the center of their attention. And Abel would play with them. The retarded one would carry his briefcase for him, and the older one would follow him into the house, begging him to show his violin to her and to explain how he played it, and the kinds of sounds it made. Sometimes, the little retarded one would throw herself on him, hugging his left leg without letting go until her mother or sister would pull her away.

But the Becerra family didn't live long in our neighborhood. One morning, without offering any explanation, they informed Mrs. Debeikis that they were moving to Germany. The husband had told me that he had been offered a position in a chemical factory that was a part of the arms industry and that his wife had gotten a job running a kindergarten. She never did like this country, she once confessed to me. To her, it seems too uncivilized, almost barbaric. The Mexicans, I remember her saying, are not only lacking in introspection but they are unpredictable, pessimistic, and given to improvisation. I later found out they paid two months in advance, packed up, and said good-bye, just like that.

Next, a young couple rented the house for four years. They moved out after a turbulent divorce. He was a Rotarian whom Abel and I never saw. She was slender, appealing, athletic, absent-minded, and more coquettish than pretty. She liked to tan herself on the roof and ride her bicycle in the park nearby. Something about her face moved me. The first thing she did upon moving into No. 58 was plant carnations and gladiolus in an earthen pot that she had purchased at the market in San Angel, and she bought fertile soil from the nursery in Coyoacán. Having been abandoned by the love of God and mankind, she told me, that's what house No. 58 needed. Even though she was small and fragile, the woman seemed like the perfect housewife. One or two months after arriving, and later enthused by the aesthetic effect of the flowers at the end of the entryway, she painted the iron gate a light blue color. Good taste, I commented to Abel, though I retracted my opinion the very next afternoon when I saw an interior decorator, one of those immature types who wears a big overcoat and constantly puffs on those Cuban cigars, pull up in a moving van, unload some huge, ugly smoke-glass mirrors, and hang them on the four walls of the master bedroom. Well, all right, to each his own, I guess. Time passed, the couple seemed to be quite happy, and this state of bliss, while unknown to neighbors, did seem pleasant. It also seemed obvious that at some point she would become pregnant but, no, she began to wither instead. Her face began to reveal that familiar expression of barrenness, so typical of infertility. Not long afterward, I learned of the divorce from Mrs. Debeikis and, once again, the house became silent.

Until this one morning at the end of October, the very same day Abel left for Europe and the Soviet Union. The doorbell rang. I opened the door and saw the old lady swaying back and forth even though she was leaning on her cane. She had come on a bus on Taxqueña Avenue and wanted to let me know that finally No. 58 had been rented. The night before they had called her brother-in-law from New York. They wanted a short-term contract, renewable monthly. The overabundance of vacant apartments in Mexico City had thrown the real estate business out of whack. The offer wasn't worth it . . . but when there's nothing else, what is one supposed to do? The person about to move gave the impression he wanted to be near the university and Coyoacán neighborhood. Maybe he was an academic. Mrs. Debeikis's brother-in-law had received a curriculum vitae and some other legal documents by mail, and the new renter was already on his way.

"The only sure thing about all this is that the renter is a foreigner," Mrs. Debeikis confessed. "A Czech."

⸻

I turned off the light and continued my vigilance. The flurry of the numbered boxes hypnotized me. Some moments passed. Mrs. Debeikis said good-bye while more boxes were being carried into the house. What did they contain? The new renter took some money out of his billfold and handed it to one of the movers. He then walked to the corner. The specter of a young, masculine person talking in the phone booth. The Czech waited until he was off the phone, then he entered the booth. He tried to make a call but apparently couldn't get through. As he returned, the movers were sitting on a bench, relaxing as they smoked their cigarettes, blowing smoke rings into the air that spread out and intertwined among themselves as if they were being guided by remote control. They had finished moving and were waiting for a tip.

I thought it strange that the van didn't even contain a desk or other necessary furniture, only a folding chair. The Czech is not to be trusted, I surmised. I remembered that a few days earlier, a department store had delivered a king-sized mattress and a refrigerator. That day at noon Mrs. Debeikis had a doctor's appointment and, since it was Tuesday and I didn't have any classes or meetings, she asked me to take care of the keys and help her with some household chores. She had also asked the plumber to come by and fix the sewer lines and a toilet in No. 58 and, finally, to take a look at my shower stall that for months had been pleading to have someone clean out the scum.

I continued spying until I got bored. I decided to watch the news on TV for a while and then go to bed. I heard the doorbell early the next morning. I thought it would be Mrs. Debeikis, but when I asked who it was, I heard a rough, scratchy, almost aphasic voice.

"Excuse me . . . I'm sorry to bother you." I smiled cordially. "I am the new tenant of house No. 58. I've tried several times. The telephone at the corner is broken and I need to make an important call. I didn't want to bother the old lady in No. 91 because I can tell it's difficult for her to get around. I'll make a request for telephone service tomorrow. I promise."

Although he had a strong accent in English, his Spanish was perfect. I opened the door and there he was. It's hard for me to describe him—language suddenly seems terribly inaccurate. He must have been about fifty-two years old, handsome, an intellectual who retained an air of melancholy. Something, an impulse, made me think to myself that if I had let him talk some more, if I had given him the time, I would have discovered his radiant wisdom. The impression I got was that he had been seasoned by unhappiness and by the ineptitude of human affairs: his face, which could be described as "ghostly" or "terrified," conveyed signs of trepidation, as if he was on the verge of an irrevocable repentance. Something made me think of the sorrowful figure of Don Quixote; all he lacked was a suit of armor, a shield, and his horse, Rocinante, I thought. After a few moments, it also occurred to me that he looked like an Iberian conquistador gone astray.

I would have wanted to tell him that in Mexico the telephone company takes years, sometimes five, even ten—to connect a new line. But I immediately remembered that in Czechoslovakia under the Communist government, the bureaucracy, despite the people's lack of conformity, has all the time in the universe.

I directed him toward the vestibule. With a gesture of feigned humility, he asked me if he could make a long-distance call. Before I could answer him, he took out a fifty-dollar bill. "It will be less, I assure you," he said. A friend had told him that there were telephone booths for calling overseas next to the market in San Angel, in Mixcoac, and in Coyoacán plaza. He had also been told, however, that it might take hours to get an overseas connection. "Keep the money until the next phone bill arrives . . . ," he added. "Then you can pay me the difference."

To acquiesce to his request, I knew, would be the beginning of one of those relationships with neighbors based on mutual favors and disagreements. So, what should I do? Opt for rudeness and discourtesy? It wouldn't have been my style and, if Abel were to learn of the incident later, he would be furious. I had no recourse but to point to the telephone. The Czech put the money next to it and closed his eyes. He opened them seconds later and began dialing. He stopped: incorrect dial. With a show of ineptness, distress, and shortness of breath, he said he would return instantly—he had to look for his address book. I smiled. Clueless as to what to do while he was gone, I went upstairs and looked out the window. I saw him cross the street and then return. At the telephone once again, he dialed and talked for some seven or eight minutes; first in English, then in Czech.

I went downstairs. He had hung up.

"Where did you learn to speak Spanish?" I asked him. "I'm amazed . . ."

"When I was young," he smiled. "I learned it when I worked in Prague as a translator and a tourist agent. But it was no heroic feat because my mother was Mexican."

"Really?" I waited for him to say something else but he didn't. "And where from in Mexico?"

"Mexico City. This very neighborhood, actually . . ."

Standing there, caught up in that situation where someone is introduced to a future colleague or friend, we talked for fifteen minutes. He told me he had just arrived from England and was tired. Prompted by the New York realtor, he said, Mrs. Debeikis had been nice enough to order a mattress from a store on Insurgentes Avenue; otherwise, he wouldn't have anything to sleep on tonight. We agreed that the colored-glass mirrors in the master bedroom were horrible. We talked about the previous renters, including the Becerra family. He then asked me if Copilco was safe. He had rented the house without knowing anything; the real estate company had only shown him a picture. Strangely enough, although he was concerned with safety, he had decided to rent the house because he liked the area. At first sight the neighborhood looked peaceful and pleasant to him, he said, like in his mother's days. I told him the Schools of Dentistry and Law are a mile away, perhaps less. San Angel has a post office and there are stores every five or six blocks. Also, there's a supermarket, Aurrera, just across the street from the Ghandi Bookstore on Taxqueña Avenue. The neighborhood association hires a permanent watchman who, every morning at 3:00 A.M. sharp, blows a whistle like a soccer referee, to let everyone know that all's well in the area. And a street sweeper cleans up every week, except during Lent, the latter part of September, and every time he decides to take off. I added that the municipality, whose offices are just south of here, has planned a Metro station on Copilco Avenue, but it's no more than that, simply a proposal. And the entire world knows that if Mexico wants to get rich, it would export unfinished proposals.

"It's curious that your house number is 85 and mine is 58," he said all of a sudden. "As I got here through Cerro del Agua Street, I noticed house numbers begin strangely with No. 32 and end with 34, and there's a number that repeats itself three times: 42."

"Yes," I responded. "One gets the impression that the engineer who numbered the area had no plan in mind."

"Or else he had a bad memory," he said.

I smiled. We would have continued talking but I excused myself. I had a class at 9:30 next morning and needed to get some sleep. I walked him to the door.

I was left with the impression that both of us had a lot to say, but we had been cut short; moreover, I remembered that he hadn't told me his name.

⸻

That night I once again became a victim of curiosity: I went to the window and saw him alone, lying down on the mattress. His lights were off, as if he didn't care whether he had electricity or not. He had placed the mattress in the middle of the bedroom. To one side, I thought I saw a typewriter and the folding chair. Even though from my window I only managed to see his multiple shadow reflected infinitely in the mirrors, I had a vivid recollection of his vague, sorrowful appearance.

He was on his back, motionless and serene, as if meditating on the re-incarnation of some celestial truth. Such spirituality, I must confess, triggered a defenseless skepticism in me. Perhaps he was a Hare Krishna. Is he inter-ested in Buddhism? A yellowed copy of the *Bahavagad Gita* in Sanskrit, left behind by the Becerras in a shelf down in the main floor (I saw it one day when Mrs. Debeikis showed me some newly painted walls in the house), came to mind. Had he found it behind a bookshelf in the study downstairs? Books are to be preserved, so I guessed he hadn't thrown it out. I remembered that just weeks earlier Abel and I were invited to dinner at the home of a concert singer who performed with the orchestra from time to time. A fat, open-minded spinster, the wife of God only knows whom, had sat down next to me and, at one point, we were talking about a Medieval mystic who had ex-perimented with unfamiliar elixirs, immersed himself in hallucinating exer-cises using psychedelic dyes and iodate paintings, and could relate to the vowels of the Bible, but not the consonants. According to this lady, the mys-tic did everything possible to acquire a perfect union with the divine. Upon hearing such nonsense, I looked at her. I now realize I didn't show much confidence in her, but I've already said it: those things seems ridiculous to me and I can't hide it. And I didn't do anything to encourage her to con-tinue either. She just let fly with her psychic hodge-podge, and there was no stopping her. The mystic, according to her, had discovered a hidden secret, a truth denied to the rest of humanity. Slightly annoyed, I answered back that having survived the beatnik era and, later, the hippie revolution, those practices were anachronistic and antimodern. The Czech, notwithstanding, was apparently still stuck in that era.

I knew that to spy on a neighbor's privacy was not right. Repeatedly, Abel had scolded me for prying into other people's lives, like the Monterey dental student, for instance. "You are the civics teacher here," he would caution me after finishing his evening practices or upon sitting down for dinner. "You, more than anyone else, have to accept the rules of modern urban life. No reason to be sticking our noses into what doesn't concern you. Be careful . . . You'll get yourself into trouble." But I didn't think there's much truth to the saying that curiosity killed the cat, either. Granted, my excuses were elusive. I responded, for instance, that we do the same thing at the theater: as audience, we are invited to stimulate our curiosity by acting as the fourth wall to a scene of illicit love or the decadence of an era, other people's lives unfold on stage right before our eyes. And this, thanks to that invisible wall.

Abel made fun of me. "The neighbors have no intention of inviting you to witness their private worlds," he murmured. "Furthermore, to confine an individual experience to the stage is to suspend it in a vacuum, isolate it in a laboratory, convert it into an object of study, which does not happen in the real world. Theater commercializes life, converts it into a consumer product. Our neighbors don't act," he was saying with irritation, "they only live."

I knew he was right. But, as when some defect or depravity eats away at our insides, I couldn't find a way to remedy it. And instead of dropping the issue, I would continue with stupid arguments. The universe is an immense theater, I would reply, and we, without ever desiring it, are simultaneously actors and spectators. "You have the mind of a novelist," he would conclude with resignation. I promised myself that I wouldn't open the curtains and spy on my fellow neighbors again, but I found it impossible. After getting home from school and whenever I had a little free time, I would find myself there, sitting in front of the window, like a meddler, obsessed with discovering other people's weakness. And the Czech, the mystery of whom we usually apply to extraterrestrial or foreigners coming from a remote, unknown land, was becoming my cup of tea, an entertaining pastime I was unable to avoid.

———

The telephone rang: it was Abel calling from Budapest. I was pleased to hear his voice, asked him how he was, and if the initial recitals had been successful. He said he broke a violin string in the middle of Symphony No. 5 by Anton Dvořák. He was forced to stop playing and quickly replaced during intermission. As for the rest of the trip, the hotels and tourist attractions were splendid, but the weather was dreadful. Even if it was early November, it had snowed on four different occasions during three days. He added that a German friend of his had given him a novel, *The Assignment* or *The Threat*, I'm not sure which, written by a Swiss author, Dürrenmatt or Jurguenmatt, about an assassination in the ruins of Al-Hakim in Egypt. The protagonist was a woman photographer that . . . I interrupted to tell him that long-distance calls should never be used to summarize plots of detective novels. We changed subjects. He had originally called to propose that we meet in Vienna during the third week of December. I would be able to join him for part of the concert tour and return home in time to begin the spring semester in early January. But I didn't feel like going and told him so. I preferred to wait in Mexico, periodically in touch with him. Disappointed, he tried to coax me into going. My excuse was that the school was going to hold some emergency teacher meetings I couldn't miss. Important matters, like future academic programs and scholarships, were to be discussed. The meetings were around Christmas time—the dates still open. But Abel insisted: "I don't know if I can endure thirty-five weeks by myself," he explained. I set him at ease, telling him what he wanted to hear. "You must make sacrifices for your music. I will be celebrating your triumphs from here."

We switched to another topic and before ending our conversation, I told him that one of the newspapers had published an article on the orchestra tour in the cultural section. The article included a picture of the orchestra director and another of him. He was pleased.

We hung up. I was tired; it had been a trying day. Was the Czech still stretched out meditating on the mysteries of the universe? I was going to check to see if he was still there, but I became involved in something else. I was so tired that I felt dizzy. I also felt bad not only for declining Abel's persistent invitation to meet him in Europe, but also for having lied to him with the unlikely excuse about school meetings in December. How could I have come up with such a thing? Had he suspected something? Why did I do it? The only explanation, the only reason that comes to . . . I was confused. In reality, his tour means a deserved vacation for me, I assured myself, a vacation for married couples. I had been missing him, it's true, but I was free, independent. And I have to admit that his tours have never been so prolonged; hence, in the beginning I felt like I had been deserted. But now I was inundated with happiness, and no responsibilities were pulling at me. I was enthralled with the solitude I had been experiencing those last few weeks. I did whatever I pleased. I would have breakfast alone. I read in bed withthe lamp on as long as I wanted. The routine rhythms of Tchaikovsky, Beethoven, and Brahms, with their recycled scales that at times would pierce my eardrums, weren't spoiling my afternoons. I didn't have to pick up Abel after his practice sessions at the university or chat aimlessly with his friends at the Café Parnasso. And if I so desired, I could even commit the sin of opening the curtains and spying . . .

Forty minutes later, I slid underneath the covers and went to sleep.

The following Tuesday I went out for a walk and to take care of some chores. I had to go to the paint shop, the tailor's, the shoe shop, and the bank. Then

I took a taxi home. Waiting for the traffic light to turn at Copilco and University avenues, I saw the Czech browsing at the magazine rack in the Salvador Allende Bookstore. He looked tired, as if he hadn't been able to go to sleep the night before. He looked unkempt: his clothes were wrinkled and his hair and beard uncombed. A fruit cart on the sidewalk blocked my vision (and his). He looked deeply absorbed in a text with illustrations. He seemed to be memorizing them and then rummaging over his errors of memorization.

Memorization—that night I spied on him. At about 8:00 in the evening, he sat down at the typewriter. Then he got up and disappeared into the darkness. A mirror reflected his body from his waist up as he went down the stairs.

Early the next morning, I saw him leave. Some time later I ran into Mrs. Debeikis. She told me she had seen him talking to the gardener and two policemen. She was sorry she had rented No. 58 to him. She sighed resignedly. "Now I'm going to have to deal with all those lawyers and accountants on Wall Street," the agency that had sent her brother-in-law the contract. "The foreigner's crazy!" she assured me. According to what she had heard, he had been in jail and in a psychiatric hospital. I couldn't believe it. The old lady had a tendency to gossip. He gave the impression of not being a hard worker; hence, it's possible that Mrs. Debeikis perceived him as lazy. I tried to calm her down.

"A crazy person in Czechoslovakia is more sane than anyone else in the world," I told her. "In Communist countries, if someone embraced antigovernment ideologies, the person would be considered demented." She wasn't satisfied and continued: "He's dirty. The house must be full of cockroaches and little balls of dirt and grime everywhere. While I was out getting some exercise this morning, I saw him practically sleepwalking as he went down Taxqueña Avenue. He was staring at the roofs of the houses. He was sweating. He made me sick!

"Did he see you?"

"No. Well, yes. He stared at my cane for a second, as if to examine it;

then he continued on without recognizing me. I still haven't received a cent for the rent."

I recommended that she be patient. Whatever the case, there hadn't yet been a better offer.

The next time I had a conversation with my neighbor it was at noon on a humid, hazy November day. We ran into each other in the park. I was getting off the bus with a load of plastic bags. He saw me and walked toward me.

"Hello. May I help?"

Again, he seemed to be possessed by some strange interior force, an energy that consumed him little by little without mercy. I deeply felt that he was suffering from a perpetual pain in his soul. I handed him the bags and we walked together. I asked him if the telephone company had finally connected his phone. He said they hadn't, but now he didn't need it so much. He had found a telephone booth with folding doors at the Faculty of Dentistry about half a mile away. He wanted to write in the mornings and would arrive by 7:00 A.M., and it was convenient to call at that early hour because of the time difference in London and Prague.

We talked about Mrs. Debeikis, who had given me her keys again and was off to the doctor with intolerable headache. The doctor was also located in the southern part of the city.

"Coyocán is fascinating," he said before saying good-bye. "The plaza, the majestic colonial church, the restaurants . . . My grandmother had a home near Viveros. I've been told that the conquistadors had their estates in this area, isn't that right? In our park, there is a commemorative plaque near the fountain explaining that on their way to Tenochtitlán, Iberian horses grazed in Copilco. And I read that during the Vice Royalty the area was a vacation spot . . ."

He marveled at the juxtaposition of historical periods, symbols, and the misery. He talked about how he has contemplated hours on end functional buildings of concrete and glass inspired by Le Corbussier and baroque churches whose exteriors are adorned with cherubim and mandrakes, as if the supreme architect, the designer of Mexico City, had deliberately played games with the intention of creating a rivalry. The past made him uneasy. He would stop people on the street and ask them questions, but very few had the answers.

"What makes Mexico so astonishing," he continued, "is that despite its rich history and centuries of aging, Mexico is a country without memories. Humble people don't even have an idea who the heroes and the villains are. Sure, they know where a certain street is or how to get to some monument dedicated to a priest or an emperor; but, that's it," to which he added: "A perfect place to lose one's memory!"

His ideas made sense. Mrs. Debeikis is wrong . . . I said to myself. He's a strange bird, a hermit. But, is he crazy? I doubt it.

He asked me what I taught at my school and if I was single. I told him that Abel was a professional musician. Then I seized the moment to introduce myself.

"And I'm Zdenek . . . Zdenek Stavchansky."

The name of a pianist or composer, I thought. He took a laminated license out of his pocket to show me the spelling of his name. The accompanying picture must have been at least ten years old. No beard, but he sported an affable grin that had disappeared with time.

"This picture was taken in Bratislava on April 7, 1969." The precision of the date amazed me.

We were at the entryway. I began to say good-bye and Zdenek asked if the telephone bill had come. "I have the feeling that $50 isn't going to be sufficient."

I smiled. "Don't worry . . . The bill will come soon enough."

I went into the house and the first thing I did was check the mail. A card from Warsaw. I turned on the answering machine. No messages. I put on my robe and slippers, and I went to the kitchen to fix a snack. While I ate, I thought about our friendly conversation on the street. Suddenly, I remembered the numbered boxes and I was surprised that I hadn't seen any of them in the trash. What did they contain? Clothes? Zdenek was always wearing the same old pants and soiled shirt. Books? That must be it . . . but, how many? Ever since the movers had come, I hadn't seen him read anything in his bedroom or at the park. At the first chance, I would ask him what they contained. I would never have guessed that almost a month would go by before the opportunity would present itself, nor would I know that by then their contents would have appeared right before my eyes.

I was tired. I washed my face and before going to bed, I went to the window. As always, the first thing I saw was total darkness; however, this time a completely different banquet was waiting for me. Little by little, I began to perceive his silhouette in a horizontal position on the mattress. His outline hardly reflected in the mirrors. He was stretched out in a strange way, it seemed so uncommon that I imagined he was a giant mollusk with an unusual agglomeration of tentacles. He's in a ghost-like, Kafkaesque state, I told myself. The bizarre, bewildering part began when I saw him stand up. He left the bedroom and, after three or four minutes, he returned with something in his hands. It was a . . . What was it? Even in the dark, it seemed like a piece of cloth with a floral design on it. Yes, it was a dress. I remained motionless and attentive behind the curtains. Zdenek sniffed it, caressed it, and he nuzzled his face in it. Why was he acting that way? A few moments later he left again and then returned with another piece of clothing. A pair of pants. Then a scarf. A handkerchief. He examined them up close and from far away. He seemed to convert them into religious fetishes. He would lay down and then get up again. Minutes later, now somewhat more at ease, he sat down in front of the typewriter and began to bang on the keys. But Zdenek didn't rest for long; he grasped the dress once again, reached for the scarf, and then closed his eyes. At that very moment he swirled around and kneeled down. He looked toward No. 85. Was he aware that I was spying on him? I think so. He has discovered me, I thought. I quickly closed the curtains and hid behind them. My heart was beating. I waited two, maybe three minutes. I went back to the window but Zdenek was out of my vision: he had gone downstairs. I looked at the clock. I had been watching him less than fifteen minutes. I could have sworn that it had been much longer.

———

I had a dream that night. A giant golden clock, surrounded by a dark cloud of ink, floated in the open space of my bedroom. Abel, wearing a long green tunic and a mask, appeared from behind a folding divider and he told me the clock belonged to Zdenek and I should return it to him immediately. I told him that I couldn't recognize him with the mask on. And if I couldn't see him, there was no reason to take him seriously. Mechanically, Abel repeated the directive. Doubtful, I decided that not to obey him would be an insult and I ran after the clock but I couldn't grasp it; each time I had it in my hands, it slipped through my fingers. I tried several times without any luck. My last attempt resulted in a fall into a swimming pool that opened up underneath the frame of the master bed. A policeman with a whistle was in the pool. When he saw me, he blew it hard.

At that moment I woke up.

———

An aunt of mine who lives in Guadalajara invited me to spend Christmas and New Year's with her. Although I wasn't up to traveling, I accepted. I bought a round-trip ticket on the train. I notified Mrs. Debeikis that I would be gone for a week or so and I put a couple of novels, a magazine, and some letters that I should answer in my suitcase. I had a good time in Guadalajara, and from there I talked to Abel, who was in Luxembourg.

While I was in Guadalajara, I was overtaken by a continual, ferocious appetite. My breakfasts were succulent and abundant. My aunt would fix lunches and dinners that in another era would have precipitated unbearable indigestion. Upon noticing how much I was eating, she asked if I was pregnant. Past unsuccessful attempts in my life made me say yes. My answer produced a pain that reached my intestines.

I returned to Copilco in early January. I took a taxi from the train station to my front door. As the suitcases were being put on the sidewalk, Zdenek came outside to help me.

"Welcome."

He was very happy to see me and said that he had missed me. He looked even more emaciated, as if he had been on a rigorous diet or were sick with cancer. His appearance was ghost-like, atrocious. Dark black circles surrounded his eyes. As usual, he hadn't combed himself. His shirt was unbuttoned and his shoes were untied. If Mrs. Debeikis were to see him now, I said to myself, she would honestly believe that a crazy man in Czechoslovakia and another in Mexico look one and the same.

"You look frail, Zdenek. Have you been eating properly? Has something happened to you?"

"Yes, I have been feeling bad. My illness is slowly getting worse. It shouldn't affect me physically, but as you can see, that's what has happened to me over the past few days. There's nothing I can do."

"What illness?"

He smiled without replying. An intuition ran through me. And what if he's really crazy? Perhaps I was wrong, but I should be careful around him.

He picked up my suitcases and carried them with the same sureness that one's permanent partner exhibits. I thanked him. I opened the door, went in, and saw that he was following behind.

"Thank you very much. I'm very tired, Zdenek . . . We'll have an opportunity to talk another time."

He apologized and left. I got the sensation he was behaving like a servant or a butler. How strange!

It occurred to me that he was a convalescent who had come to Mexico City to die. From the window that night I saw him stretched out again. I decided that he wasn't meditating. No. Zdenek was concentrating on a precise, particular point in space; hence, I eliminated his possible Buddhist affiliation. Later that night, as on other nights, I discovered that he had perfected his nightly theatrical routine; his libretto was detailed and meticulous: first, he dressed up in miner's gear (boots, piolet, and lantern) and pretended to beat on someone; then he'd make a fire and be a Boy Scout with a Sir Baden Powell cap, ruffled shirt, and camping equipment. His performances included mimicking a cook (with apron) and, finally, imitating a male nurse (with gown and stethoscope) who saves a drowned person or a boxer. I guessed that the major part of his wardrobe and props came from the cardboard boxes. Between presentations, he would spend hours sniffing pieces of cloth or examining photographs that he would take out of other boxes. He would show peculiar expressions and act incomprehensibly. When he would mimic the chef, he would also argue with some stranger, mix some kind of liquid, or take a bite out of an apple. Each change of clothes represented a distinct change in Zdenek as he enacted diverse scenes in different contexts. And at the end of his routine, he would sit down at the typewriter and, although he didn't seem capable of producing more than a poor, unfortunate paragraph, he would make an effort to write a text, explain something, or narrate something imaginary.

I confess that as the nights went by (and there weren't that many), I felt afraid. Mrs. Debeikis was right: he'd lost his marbles. Should someone call the police? How should I act when I'm around him? Was he aggressive? Dangerous? But there were other more immediate questions: What did he live on? Perhaps he would receive checks in the mail. What was he doing here in Mexico City? To lose one's memory, I remember he had said. Abel in Europe and me here alone . . . the loneliness and freedom I was enjoying turned sour.

If he is crazy, I said to myself, he still has certain habits that are not typical of someone who has gone loony. According to the way he behaved, to imagine he was suffering from some abnormality was not very convincing. Our conversations were friendly and pleasant. Zdenek was inoffensive, sane, and sensible; perhaps his past included some unbearable tragedy or depraved romance. With so much mystery, I felt I had become an integral part of a detective adventure whose clock-like mechanisms were about to overtake me. The only thing I knew with any certainty, it's true, was that something profound yet unidentifiable attracted and exasperated me about my hermetic neighbor.

It occurred to me suddenly that he must be an actor, a failed one at that. I remembered an old story by Juan Carlos Onetti, a Uruguayan writer, about a spurious businessmen who goes crazy a long ways from Buenos Aires and is hired by a rich, bourgeois female to present a happy dream she had experienced years earlier. Zdenek must have been an actor who was possessed by the costumes of his past, the roles he played, and the characters he represented on the stage. His part was to be theatrical; mine, to be his audience. Yes, he knew I would watch him. He performed for me. He amused himself with me. He knew I was there watching and he took advantage of the opportunity to show his talent. He was the puppeteer—the creator—and, simultaneously, his own puppets; he was the owner of a Guignol Theater inside of which I had become trapped. I got frightened, I became furious.

Near the end of January or at the beginning of February, Mrs. Debeikis called to say she still had not received any rent money for No. 58. "What I would give to have more renters like you people!" she said. "The Czech is a charlatan." Since she wasn't on the best of terms with her brother-in-law, she hadn't had the opportunity to notify him of what had happened. She decided to wait a little longer.

On an afternoon off from work, I took a walk. I sat down on a bench at the park. Shortly thereafter, I heard footsteps. Zdenek was practically on top of me. We greeted each other. He sat down next to me.

"For some months now, I've been watching you spy on me," he said. No answer would have been equally disconcerting.

"How embarrassing!" I responded, cheeks turning red. "A lack of discretion . . . Really, I'm quite inhibited. But I sleep lightly . . . Abel calls it 'susceptibility'." I had to lie to him. Any kind of noise wakes me up: snoring, a squeaking door, or dripping water . . . I don't know what to do during those long hours of insomnia."

"Some time back I was offended. I have grown accustomed to having you as a spectator."

Zdenek had taken me by surprise. Better to assume a position of honesty and simply contend with it. "I spy on you very little . . . Moreover, you hardly ever turn on the lights."

"Darkness is perfect for the memory because it's free of the upheavals of daytime madness."

"What do you keep in those boxes?" I asked. "Clothes? Photographs? I've watched you take out things that look sentimental."

"Exactly," he said. "Sentimental and memorable."

"I apologize," I responded. "I shouldn't have stuck my nose into things.

While Abel is away, I'm going to sleep downstairs. That way I won't be tempted to . . ."

Zdenek wasn't paying any attention to what I was saying. "Your husband, where is he now?"

"Prague. He'll be on his way to Vienna in two days. Perhaps on Monday . . ."

"It's almost an unbelievable place: it belongs less to its millions of inhabitants than to the restrained Jew, Franz Kafka. And tell me, is this the first time he . . . ?"

"No," I smiled. "His tours take him to Czechoslovakia every two years. Sometimes, even more frequently."

"I lived north of Vaclavske Namesti. Quite far from the Hebrew cemetery. I'm from Karlovyvary, a tourist town located between Vienna and Prague that's famous for its sulfur hot springs, a place where in times past the noble class took medicinal baths and enjoyed themselves by relaxing."

"What brought you to Mexico?"

He laughed heartily. "I already told you: to lose my memory . . ."

Given that he was perhaps dangerous, I didn't want to insist. "The telephone bill arrived several weeks ago."

"How much did the call cost?"

"I don't remember offhand, but I'll let you know."

After that we about other trivial topics. Then we said good-bye.

✎────

I prepared my class, turned on the TV, and tried to correct some exams. It was 8:30 in the evening. The temptation to go to the window swelled inside me. No, resign yourself. Abel. Shouldn't he have called today? And what if I try to get him in Prague? I opened the telephone book and looked for the country code. I flipped feverishly through the pages. No luck. My mind was on other things. I decided, then, to cross the street and ask Zdenek himself. It's a ridiculous excuse, I know, but the telephone bill would be a stratagem.

I rang the doorbell. Zdenek came to the door.

"Am I bothering you? I checked the bill and your call cost $43.25. If you want, I can return the $50 bill and you can pay me the equivalent in pesos."

"Please, come in . . . ," he responded, ignoring my words once again.

"Thank you, but I have a lot to do. In fact, I would like to ask you how to dial Prague. I want to call Abel and . . ."

He went down to the entryway and opened the door.

"Come in."

I accepted his invitation almost against my own will and went into his living room. I discovered that the walls were bare and, just like Mrs. Debeikis had predicted, there were balls of lint and dirt in the corners. There was nothing in the room except for all those boxes piled up everywhere, a jacket, and some airmail envelopes. There wasn't even a place to sit down. Such an unfriendly environment . . . I felt obliged to smile.

"Coffee or tea."

I answered and Zdenek disappeared into the kitchen. I thought it was incredible that after five months he still had no furniture. I heard the rattling of dishes and the stove being lit. I went over to some boxes. The numbering on them was confusing. They were still closed with adhesive tape. I touched one.

"Open it!" I turned around and Zdenek was leaning against the door sill.

"Any one of them, it doesn't matter which," he added.

He was playing with my curiosity. I got frightened. Should I obey him? And what if he's crazy? Something could happen over which I would have no control. I doubted my reasoning, but I thought: if I'm already in his house, it's probably better to see this through. I tore off the tape on No. 109, and opened it. Just as I had thought: there were packages of photographs, a book, articles of clothing, a pair of old sandals, an umbrella, a purse decorated with sea shells, and other things like the ones Zdenek had been using in his nocturnal performances.

Looking into his penetrating eyes, I felt naked. The pot of water must have been boiling because he turned around and disappeared.

"Are you an actor?" I yelled toward the kitchen.

Another hearty laugh.

Moments later the door to the kitchen opened. I saw him enter the room with two steaming ceramic cups, a pewter sugar bowl, and some napkins.

"Do you mind if we sit on the floor?" he asked. "I don't have a sofa and every morning I get up telling myself to at least buy some folding chairs. I have one upstairs in the bedroom. If you would like . . ."

"This is fine, thanks."

He poured me a cup of tea. Each one of us found a place to sit.

"What's the purpose of so much old clothing?"

"Old things speak to us, they attract and reject us. Besides, you have seen me sniffing these articles of clothing, losing myself in them. It's a memory technique."

Once again, I was irked by his aloofness; thus, I decided to change the subject.

"Should I give you the $6.75 change in Mexican pesos?"

"However you want." He stared at the boxes. "I'm ill and Mexico has always represented the last frontier for me, it's a geography without a map. Perhaps I've come here to die . . ." I was horrified. I told him not to talk like that, for he was still young. "I'm suffering from a curious, unexplainable, and incurable illness . . . an unremitting illness."

"What do you do?"

"Right now? Recuperate lost memory, like Proust."

"And in Prague?"

"I was a professional in memory recovery, a mnemonist. Until 1968 . . .

Do you know what a mnemonist does? Have you ever heard of Ishihara of Japan, Irineo Funes of Uruguay, Vladimir Sharashevsky of Russia?"

"No."

"A mnemonist supports himself remembering, making his memory work for him."

"Are you a Jew?" It was a stupid question and I corrected myself: "Jews have good memories. Abel has several Jewish colleagues in the orchestra."

"I had a good memory. But amnesia has been eating away at it." Again he looked at the boxes. "They were full of photographs and memoranda."

He stood up. He took a picture out of one of the boxes. He showed it to me. "Vaclavske Namesti, September 18, 1964. That's me. They paid me to participate in the Party's social gatherings. The guests gave me lists of fifty or sixty numbers. I would memorize them and then repeat them first in ascending and then in descending order.

"Impossible." He took a pen from the lone jacket and looked for a piece of newspaper in a nearby closet. As he gave them to me, he spoke with unbefitting pride. "The most studied type of regressive lost memory," he said, "is the one in which the limbic system is most affected, including the temporal lobes. It's a delirious encephalopathy (it's called Wernicke's Disease) that is caused by a deficiency of thiamin or Vitamin B1. The doctors have a name for it: Korsakoff's Syndrome. The Russian neurologist Sergei Korsakoff was born in 1854 and died in the late 1800s. His diagnosis, in the case of alcohol abuse, was always correct."

He looked straight at me. "This will be a free demonstration." He put the newspaper and the pen in front of me. "Write down fifty numbers. Each number can have up to four digits, let's say, 12, 1467, 255 . . . Whatever you want. You can repeat numbers as well."

I felt confused. I wrote down the following list of numbers:

754, 12, 548, 1003,
7809, 989, 111, 54,

```
32, 2056, 908, 412,
101, 25, 9887, 139,
15, 873, 2003, 777,
5690, 89, 987, 101,
412, 5430, 28, 479,
5690, 909, 612, 98,
11, 7098, 887, 532,
82, 105, 7680, 431.
```

He asked me if I was ready. I said yes. He asked me to read them out loud at three-second intervals. He also asked me not to pronounce any other words while I was reading the numbers, for he would remember them as well. I began. While I read, Zdenek leaned back and looked at the ceiling. He assumed the same horizontal position that he always took when he stretched out on the mattress in the master bedroom. When I had finished, he waited a few minutes and then looked at me. I'll repeat them in reverse order, he said. He did it without a single error and then he repeated them in the order that they were originally read: 754, 7809, 32, 101, 15, 5690 . . .

His feat left me dumbfounded, hypnotized. But when he got to 612, he stopped; it seemed as if he had become immersed in a cold sweat. He tried 857 and went on to 897. He closed his eyes again. he tried in vain to remember the number. His impatience became evident. He went on to the next numbers: 7680, 1003 . . . but he erred in 777 and 98. Then he was finished. He was exhausted. He used to have a prodigious memory, he said, sighing. But I'm slowly losing it. It's Korsakoff's Syndrome, but an irregular type.

I didn't know what to tell him, so I didn't say anything. "When I was a child, my mother Miriam was fascinated and proud of my vast memory. Before going to the market, she would sit me down in a chair in the kitchen. She would open the refrigerator door or the cupboards and name the things that were lacking. I would memorize them and at the market I would restate the list the way I had memorized it. She would purchase the items and when she believed she had everything she needed, she would ask me to repeat the list. My talent for memory is synthetic, it's based on photographic imagery. The numbers that you read to me were perceived as images in my mind, the same way I would see the items that my mother needed for the market.

The tea was getting cold. I took a sip. I looked at him like a servant who looks at his master: captivated, possessed. He added that learning languages had been easy for him. He spoke Russian, Yiddish, Polish, English, French, Italian, and, naturally, Czech and Spanish. He simply memorized dictionaries. His syntax, however, was clumsy. He had perfected it when he did translations and worked as a tourist guide. The Government gave him the position because no one else could remember the size of Czechoslovakia (49,370 square miles), the birth and death of the first presidents (Thomas Garrigue Masaryk and Eduard Benes), the date of the Munich Pact (1938), the ancient rivalries among Moravia, Bohemia, and Slovaquia, the Second World War, the Occupation, the details of Maharal of Prague and his fantastic creature, the Golem, the total number of graves in the Hebrew cemetery, the architectural design of the Alterschule, etc.

"I came because Mexico is the land of my maternal ancestors, it's true. It's the uterus. But also because it's a Land of Promise and a Land of Oblivion. In Mexico history is cyclic: nothing ever vanishes; it's only eclipsed. Yesterday and tomorrow are one and the same and the present its eternal. This is a geography where the European and the American memories have clashed in an epic battle. Here nobody remembers. Or better, everybody forgets to remember. I have followed what goes on here since I was very little and I feel I know the people. I am intimately related to this land." As he talked, he tore the adhesive tape from box No. 56 and removed a packet of pictures tied together with a yellow ribbon. He untied it and examined the images. He turned them over to look at some information written on the back. Then he closed his eyes and sighed. What were those photographs about? Why did he care for them so much? I thought of the many performances

Zdenek had staged for me in the window. The content of the pictures was an inspiration. He had been acting for me in order to remember his past, to reenact his memories. I was his audience and he expected some sort of applause for the show. What was the real meaning of his stage acts? I suddenly felt I cared for him. Abel, his life, his music, were a part of my discontinued past. They lacked the feeling of passionate adventure. Our love was domestic, peaceful, routine. Zdenek, on the other hand . . . I restrained myself. My incipient disloyalty made me feel ashamed.

I looked at my watch. One thirty-five in the morning. Tomorrow was Friday. My first class was at nine sharp. But some inner light, a hidden certainty, stimulated me to let Zdenek hug me, to lose myself in him. It might seem like nonsense, but I am at a loss to remember in any detail what happened after that moment. I've erased it from my mind, as if it never happened. But it did, there's no doubt about it. It happened, because, two, maybe three, hours later, I got up. I felt like I had been led astray, as if someone had erased from my mind any evidence that by just crossing the street . . . could I find No. 85, my own house? I had lost my will power. I was a puppet. Zdenek's epidermis, the warmth of his breath, were all over me. Inside me. I was dizzy and frightened. I saw my hand reach out and touch his cheek. I wanted to run away. His body and mine floated on an ocean of old clothes and yellowed photographs of strange people. We wallowed in memories.

I was feverish. I hardly slept. I imagined that every minute the phone was going to ring. Abel would be calling and recognize the nervousness in my voice. Later on in the night, I returned in a taxi. I was afraid to cross the street with Zdenek. I had no idea what to do.

I couldn't control my wandering mind. And what if Zdenek's story had been one big lie, a trick in order to hypnotize me, the magic of a madman? Undoubtedly, it was his story. He had captivated me. I felt . . . that I had been raped? I remembered Mrs. Debeikis. Why hadn't she asked the Czech for the rent money? It wasn't any concern of mine. I needed to relax. I was tired. I wanted to take a bath. I turned on the tap and the gushing water fascinated me. Thousands of millions of drops streamed past me. This would be the only moment that we would share with each other. I had a terrible headache. I went down to the kitchen and took an aspirin. I went back upstairs and got into the oceanic serenity of the bathtub.

Unexpectedly, I heard the phone ring. I got frightened. Was it Abel? My heart was beating. And what if it was Zdenek? Impossible. He didn't have my number. I won't answer. Ignore it. My colleagues at school had noted my nervous behavior, and I shouldn't let Abel suspect anything. Maintain my composure. To discover my uneasiness could affect him and upset his musical concentration. The telephone stopped ringing and I waited. Mollified and drowsy, I was in reverie: the water was uterine and gentle. The silence was imponderable, supernatural, irrational. How much time . . . had passed? Half an hour? Less, perhaps.

Now it was the doorbell. Someone was knocking. I became frightened again. A woman all alone in Mexico City . . . hardly the best situation. Who could it be? It had to be Zdenek. No, I'm not going to the door. I'm staying in the tub, motionless, in silence, for as long as it takes. What time could it be? It must have been close to ten thirty at night. It was late for someone to come to visit. The doorbell rang again, and again, and again. I waited a few more minutes. Whoever it was, they would have to give up. I was exhausted. I got out of the tub, put my robe on, and wrapped my hair in a towel.

I lay down on the bed. Two hours later, I felt ponderous but more serene. I put on my pajamas and turned out the light.

I was awakened by the deafening cry of an ambulance siren. I got the impression it was right in front of my house. I heard voices, people were talking. I saw a patrol car. Three policemen were talking while one reported the incidents on the car radio. I saw Zdenek. He watched everything from the other side with terrifying passivity. I looked for my slippers and robe. I passed by the mirror. I had gone to sleep with wet hair and it was uncombed. I looked like an ostrich. I dampened my hair in the sink and combed it.

I went outside. Two ambulance attendants were preparing a stretcher in the ambulance. The door to Mrs. Debeikis' house was open and a policeman was hurrying inside. Perhaps it's a heart attack, someone murmured who saw me nearby. I couldn't believe it. Her brother-in-law had called 911, said his friend. I was astonished. Some attendants came out of No. 91 with a stretcher. Mrs. Debeikis was covered with a sheet. One of the young men, shouting that he needed something from the first-aid kit, carried the old cane in one of his hands.

———

The wake was held at a funeral home on Churubusco Avenue. Her sister the florist, her husband, and her brother-in-law, who had helped her take care of her properties, were there. Also, her daughter, son-in-law, and granddaughter, who had grown considerably since the last time I had seen her, had flown in from Hartford, Connecticut.

Death, its immanence, its leveling appetite, has always made me terribly afraid. To stand in front of Mrs. Debeikis's corpse was like falling into an abyss. I had just talked with her a few days ago and now . . . she was lifeless, absent of volition. Zdenek's mnemotechnic theories came to mind. Facing a loved one, he would have said, one's memory resists accepting that our mental movie of a certain person has to end.

The wake was replete with a sad crowd. I offered my condolences. I felt loathsome, a secret accomplice to the death of the old lady. According to the police, Mrs. Debeikis had called her brother-in-law, who lives in Satelite, on the other side of the city. And, in turn, he had tried to call me. Could I have saved her? Perhaps. If I had hurried. Her brother-in-law had called other neighbors but no one answered. Abel is accustomed to saying that when it comes to emergencies, everyone is busy.

I attended the funeral a few days later. People asked about Abel. I explained that he was on tour. We talk with each other from time to time, I added. I told them I missed him. It was a lie. I felt like I was talking about a stranger. I had changed. I was someone else. I was wearing a mask.

"What's going to happen to No. 91?" I asked the old lady's brother-in-law at one point. He responded that he'd probably sell the property along with No. 58. The Czech still hadn't paid his rent and the lawyers will end up throwing him out. I inquired if he was inclined to sell No. 85. "I doubt it," he responded. "You people have been good renters . . . moreover, given that Nos. 91 and 58 are separated by only a wall, if they're sold together, they'll make a great piece of property for something else."

As I walked along Taxqueña Avenue toward the bus stop after the funeral, I ran into the Copilco neighborhood watchman, the one who blows his whistle at 3:30 in the morning like a soccer referee. He said he had been looking for me. It was that time of month to pay him. Without wincing one bit, he reminded me we hadn't given him a Christmas bonus like in previous years. I asked him to come around to the house later or another day. He wasn't friendly. Before leaving, he told me that the neighbor in No. 58, the foreigner, had been looking for me. Something about the telephone.

⸻

The following week I went into seclusion. I felt bad, remorseful. I closed the windows and shut the curtains. I didn't want to know anything about the outside world. I read novels, listened to records, skimmed newspapers. I cooked only when I felt like eating. Abel called a couple of times, once from Moscow. I told him that Mrs. Debeikis had died. He was sorry. He said he would dedicate the next concert to her. Deep inside me I was pleased to have gone through all this without Abel. I enjoyed my solitude, but I knew that I had been hypocritical because an inner force, one against which I fought foolishly, propelled me toward Zdenek. I didn't allow myself to spy on him. I didn't even allow myself to talk to him. Every time I would go out, I devised ways to avoid being seen. Who had rung my doorbell that night? I thought that the mystery would be resolved if he would ring it again one of these days.

He never did.

One afternoon near the end of my seclusion, a dry, foul-smelling smoke filled the air as if someone in the neighborhood was burning plastic or garbage. Perhaps some vagrant had made a fire in the park, I said to myself. It happens when the street sweeper doesn't show up for work.

My seclusion came to an end the second Sunday of March. I was tired of being isolated, so I decided to take a walk in Coyoacán Plaza. I couldn't continue to run away from Zdenek. As I was leaving for the market, I noticed that the door to No. 58 was open. Something had changed. The house was empty. A realtor was showing it to a potential buyer.

An indescribable sensation overtook me; it was as if I had been made useless. Zdenek has left, I told myself. He's abandoned me. He left without saying good-bye. I remembered the night the movers were sitting on a bench smoking cigarettes while they waited to get paid. I remembered the scene, and a burning sensation, an immense feeling of rage, crept upwards from deep inside my stomach. I wanted to hit someone or something, destroy everything around me. I felt like vomiting. I went toward the door. What kind of buyers would be interested in this place? I heard the realtor say something about the mirrors in the master bedroom. They discussed the eventuality of a metro stop being constructed in Copilco, which would probably attract renters. I entered the house. I walked into the living room. Not a trace of the boxes. What had Zdenek done with his theater of memory? I went out into the garden and observed that the grass was covered with a thin layer of ashes. I went closer. The remains of the fire covered the area. In one corner there was a pile of burned remains: a lantern, a boot, a stethoscope, a piolet, an apron, etc. Impossible! Zdenek had burned the contents of the boxes! I remembered the penetrating smell of a couple of days ago. He had given up. And his book of memories? Would he finish it some day? It pained me to think that among the many millions of inhabitants of Mexico City, no one in this giant labyrinth was capable of making contact with this Czech. Once again, I remembered the similarity between Don Quixote and him. No one else will remember him, I thought. I smiled. He had chosen Mexico in order to erase the last traces of his memory. An excellent decision, I murmured. After all, this is the Olympus of Forgetfulness. Here, no one remembers anything. Everything is erased, nothing remains. With the thousands of daily abuses and atrocities, infinite, individual stories are devoured by an immense, monstrous, raging crater that is at the same time everyone and no one.

I heard sounds. The realtor and the client had come down the stairs and were entering the living room.

"I'm the neighbor from across the way," I said. "No. 85. I didn't know this house was up for sale. Well, I knew it was but I didn't think anyone would be interested in buying it. What I'm trying to say is . . ."

"It was rented until recently," added the realtor.

"Yes, I knew the Czech who rented it. A wise man but he was sick. The owner was Mrs. Debeikis. She lived . . ."

". . . in No. 91, the house next door," noted the client. "This gentleman is considering the possibility of acquiring both properties. Perhaps he will build . . ."

I stopped listening because I wasn't interested. What kinds of new renters would invade Copilco? Will we have workers and builders in front? Abel's cherished tranquillity will be disturbed once again, not by a rebellious, abusive young dental student but by jack hammers and saws. I remembered the times when the perfect housewife lived there before Zdenek. Perfect until she got divorced. What could have happened to her? My curiosity had been reduced to her life when she and her husband lived in No. 58. What happened to my neighbors once they had abandoned me? The Becerra family and their retarded child . . . what good was it to have known them? Was there any sort of mission in our encounter? Human history is replete with an annoying quantity of acts that serve no purpose whatsoever.

I said good-bye, not without thinking that perhaps I should be the one to buy this house—an absurd idea, no doubt: with what money? As I was walked out approaching the front door, I saw one lonely box. "A gift," I thought to myself. "Zdenek has left it for me." He wouldn't have left without . . . I became happy and, foolishly, opened it. It was empty, of course! I looked at it closely, saddened, trying to recreate a certain touch, a sigh.

TRANSLATED BY DICK GERDES

THE DEATH OF YANKOS

Gulp! — I REMEMBER THIS SOUND AS IF IT JUST HAPPENED. IT WAS A strange sound, the consummation of the bizarre journey that ended in Yankos's sad and peculiar death.

Yankos was a close friend of mine. We met in high school and since those early days of our relationship I can't forget his constant sneezing. Everybody in school thought he was allergic to flowers, newspapers, certain foods, or something. But it wasn't the case. Teachers always granted him permission to go to doctors every other week, but his disease was so rare that no diagnosis could be made. In the end, it was assumed that he suffered from the metaphysical distortion of measurement. Exactly what that is I still don't know, but nobody, as far as I am concerned, ever suffered from something similar.

I have tried to recount this story elsewhere, more than once. I failed because I never understood it entirely. The "metaphysical distortion of measurement" is by itself ridiculous. But Yankos's story was true; it happened in time and space, and it is disrespectful to assume otherwise. That is why I am now giving my telephone number—at the same time to honor my friend and to explain things further, if needed: 537-3342. If anyone is skeptical after reading my account, please call me. I may not give convincing answers. I remain skeptical myself, but we can join forces.

About a month before Yankos passed away, I saw him walking on the sidewalk of Avenida Pinocchio. He was thin, pale, and nervous. His eyes were red. It was the first time we met after seven or eight years. After graduation, although living in the same city, Caracas, we decided to split. I became an accountant and he wanted to apply to medical school. He couldn't because of the constant impediments the disease inflicted upon him. I remembered him somehow short, and seeing him again was an opportunity to verify my recollection: now he seemed even shorter. If standing in a crowd, Yankos could easily be stepped on. Never was he so short—and this was evidently another symptom of his fatal disease. When greeting him, I had to reach far down to touch his hand.

That same day he told me his father, a scholar in medieval art, had died a few months earlier, of cancer, and that he was deeply saddened. He felt apathetic, so when I asked him to come and have supper together with me and Alison, my future wife, he refused. It's not that he was rejecting my invitation. His feelings, Yankos assured me, forced him to evade social reunions.

The conversation took less than three minutes. Close to the end, I realized that Yankos's nose was somehow flat, but I didn't pay much attention to the peculiarity. After a short while we said goodbye and departed.

Two days later, as I was watching television, mindless, the phone suddenly rang: 537-3342. I answered and it was Yankos's voice. "I've been looking for you everywhere, Noam," he said. "I need you desperately. If only you will help me. That day we met on Avenida Pinocchio, do you remember? Well, after I shook your hand I knew that only you I could trust. I've chosen you, Noam, because I want you to be my last and final confessor." I didn't understand what was going on. "What happened, Yankos?" I said.

His answer was direct: "Quickly, come to my house. Come as fast as you can! I think I'm dying." Before saying goodbye he dictated his address.

Still today I don't know why he selected me to witness his decay. He lived approximately seven miles away in a small, ugly, one-bedroom apartment located in the Bellavista neighborhood, near an old bridge. An old carpet, a table, and three chairs were the only furniture.

Before going any further in describing what happened next, I must say I never leave my place without my precious die. It's a small, blue die, with points in black, a present from my grandfather. I generally have it in my right-hand pocket, but it can happen that I find it in the left-hand one. I play with it between my fingers nervously. It's therapy: it helps me to keep calm on difficult occasions.

I wanted to take a taxi to Yankos but I couldn't find one. So I walked. As I entered his apartment, I saw him lying on the floor, completely horizontal. He looked at me with surprise. His face was white and I could swear he had shortened several inches. He was constantly sneezing. "What is wrong?" I asked. "Can't you see?" he responded. "Look, the ceiling is descending."

"What?"

"My ceiling is descending," he corrected. "Not yours but mine. Look up! If you think the ceiling keeps an architectural proportion with the rest of the room, you're wrong!"

"I don't get it," I replied while playing anxiously with my die.

"Look up, Noam. Yesterday the ceiling was one inch higher. Can you believe it? It has been descending one inch every day. I feel trapped. I can't breathe. I just realized this morning: in a few days I'll be the content of a sandwich made between the floor and the stupid ceiling."

I couldn't but laugh. How can the ceiling descend? I looked around. Everything in the apartment seemed normal. The walls were in their proper places. The objects in the room kept their normal proportions. Either Yankos was joking or he was losing his mind.

"Frankly, I don't understand," I said. He sneezed again. While lying horizontal, Yankos seemed tense, his body incapable of movement. I realized once more that his nose was flat, even more than when I saw him in Avenida Pinocchio. Flat, as if compressed by some external force. My die was dancing rapidly.

"The distance between our eyes and the ceiling," Yankos continued, "although uniform for all, is different. My father said it as he was dying. . . . The sky is always the limit and everybody keeps a different proximity with the limit."

"Yankos, there's nothing strange here."

"The sky is the limit, Noam. The sky is the limit." He repeated that sentence ten or more times. Then he sneezed again.

"Why don't you stand up?" I said. "I can't," Yankos replied. "There is no space in this room for me to stand. Can't you see my nose, Noam? It's flat."

"That I know. So go to the doctor. Perhaps a doctor could help you. He could give you medicine. An anti-depressive pill or something. You may be depressed because of your father's death. Your flattened nose could be a symptom of . . . Everything will be all right, Yankos. Have some confidence."

"I can't, Noam."

What could I do? I gave him an aspirin, that's all. We talked a bit more about his miserable state. He stubbornly believed the ceiling was descending. Even as I was leaving Yankos never stood up.

Two weeks later the same situation: 537-3342. The phone rang while I was watching television. The conversation had the same tone—"I need you, Noam. . . . Please, come soon. . . ." I took my gabardine out (I thought it was raining), put my die in my right-hand pocket, and went to Yankos.

When I arrived in the Bellavista neighborhood, he was lying on his floor again, this time more tense. "Look," Yankos said. "The ceiling is lower. It has descended half the way. I am worried, Noam. What am I going to do?"

"Did you see the doctor?" I interrupted.

"Yes."

"And?"

"The doctor laughed. He spoke for ten minutes. He gave me a prescription. Eye-drops. Eye-drops. This isn't a sight problem. I told him that my nose hurts but he didn't know what else to say. It's horrible: the ceiling will end up killing me and nobody can do a thing."

I looked up at the ceiling. No change. "You are crazy, Yankos," I said. "How am I standing?"

His nose was a disaster, almost one-dimensional. I wanted to understand but I couldn't. With my die I was trying to overcome the absurdity of the scene.

"I can't stand, Noam. Altitude is individual. We are on one planet but in multiple worlds."

"Go to hell!" I joked.

"Don't get me wrong, friend!" he replied.

"Go to the doctor again."

"What for?" And Yankos sneezed again, this time even stronger.

I am no psychologist. It must be clear by now. Why should I be one? Every person has to deal with his individual problems. Why should I get mixed up in somebody else's life? Individuality was created so that men would understand their limits. Individuality is a challenge, and I wasn't going to involve myself in Yankos's life. He may have felt angry with me. I am sorry! I couldn't understand and there is nothing I could have done at the moment. So this time I left without goodbye.

537-3342. Two weeks later I went there a third time. I had received the telephone call as always, when watching television. I put on my gabardine (once more I thought it was raining) and decided to take a bus. While standing at the bus station, I saw two identical children standing close to their mother. They were smiling, as if happy for being who they were. The expression on their two faces, fresh, joyful, made me understand their inner lives, both together and each separately. They were twins. The same genetic heritage, same blood, but two bodies. One of the children was shorter. To listen to his mother, he needed to incline twice as far as his taller brother. Yankos's existential paradox surprisingly became evident to me. He could be right: the sky is located as far as each of us can reach, and also the ceiling. Never before did I realize it and now, after this epiphany, I slightly understood my friend's sickness. "Mmm. . . ." Yankos is getting shorter, farther from the limit. To a certain point, each of us has his own sky. To a certain degree, each of us lives in his own three-dimensional universe. "What an insight!" I said to myself. "Mmm. . . . Insights are a product of pure chance."

Yankos, again, lay horizontal in his apartment. It was obvious in his nose that he was dying. He was even shorter. He looked like a dwarf. The dimensions of his universe didn't allow him to live any longer. The ceiling was so close, and yet so far. "Everybody's sky is everybody's limit," I repeated for my own. "Is there a reasonable explanation for Yankos's fatal disease?"

We started talking about diverse subjects, metaphysics among them. I wanted to tell Yankos about my epiphany. I was willing to acknowledge that now I understood a little more, that Yankos's sickness was somehow less obscure to me. But I couldn't. Evading the subject, he talked about his late father, about our years in school, about his nose, and other "stupid" (this was Yankos's own adjective) things. My die was dancing in my pocket as never before. "You must fight, Yankos. Nobody can be flattened by the ceiling. Nobody can die of a metaphysical distortion of measurement."

It was now that he unexpectedly sneezed. He hadn't sneezed before during this, our final encounter, and as he did so the volume of his body was instantaneously lost. Rapidly my friend became part of that morbid environment. He, on the old carpet, became the carpet. He, in that apartment, became the apartment. Just one second and his life became a sandwich between ceiling and floor. The phenomenon was astonishing. He had been three-dimensional . . . and, then, Yankos was completely flat, a piece of paper. Yankos's shadow and himself were one.

By reflex, I saw my gabardine on one of the chairs. I had placed it there when I arrived. A normal size. I looked up: the ceiling, my ceiling, kept a normal position. "Can ceilings descend?" I wanted to ask Yankos. "Mmm. . . ." But it was too late. He was dead and nothing could be done.

Astonished as I was, I introduced my helpful little die into my mouth and swallowed—Gulp!

TRANSLATED BY THE AUTHOR

THE ONE-HANDED PIANIST

For Danilo Kiš

AS SHE WOKE UP YESTERDAY, SHE KNEW GOD WAS IN THE KITCHEN. IT was one of those indescribable insights that would take possession of her, and which, somehow or other, she had gotten used to shaking off. Her intuition told her, indeed, that this time God was there to be found. That if she were to get out of bed to look for him she would find Him. Not in human form, though. She would sense His presence in a scent, in the strong scent of a pine tree. Should she get up? How many times would she wake up in pain and later realize that the pain didn't actually exist? How many times had her own insights lied to her? At least now her bedclothes were protecting her. To go or not to go. She couldn't decide. Sure, she could go downstairs and verify that it was all a hoax, that such a smell didn't exist. Or, she could remain in bed.

"God doesn't exist." Esdras said that God doesn't exist. At least not the omnipotent, merciless God of violent religions, the Almighty that gives and takes away without any explanation. "There's another one," he affirmed, "that exists in objects, in details, in the things that no one pays attention to.

For example, the smell of an olive tree . . ." And Malvina had been waiting for weeks, perhaps even months, for Him to appear. Her God.

She knew the feeling of waking up and knowing that He was reachable in the kitchen. It was a rainy morning in October, months before the accident involving her mother and stepfather, Esdras. She was alone, as always. Was there ever a time when she hadn't been? She knew God was waiting for her, that He would be there until she met Him face-to-face. It was 4:30 in the morning, or close to it. The noise the raindrops were making on the window frames was scaring Malvina—poor thing!, a young woman like her, so alone in such an empty house. She turned on the lights and remained silent. She couldn't decide what to do then, either. She didn't want to go downstairs in vain, nor did she want to miss a chance.

She missed it because she was careless. It had taken her too long to put on her robe and slippers, and by the time she reached the kitchen, it was already too late. The only thing she smelled was the strong scent of dishwashing liquid. She was furious. . . . It should never happen again.

Malvina was a stutterer and had difficulty concealing the problem. She would trip over syllables that contained *t*'s and *r*'s, *c*'s and *r*'s, or *p*'s and *r*'s. She couldn't pronounce words like "t-t-triangle," "c-c-r-redit," "c-c-crater," or "p-p-procreation." Everyone laughed at her and she felt ridiculed, embarrassed, inadequate, and hated to talk because, even though she didn't intend to, she always came across one of those tricky words that announced her verbal disability.

Every six months or so, she would hear another theory explaining her defect. She would hear them from specialists and doctors she visited. One of them attributed the problem to the fact that in the mother's uterus, a genetic code had decided that Malvina's embryo was going to be left-handed and at the last minute there had been a change, a hesitation. Why? One of

Nature's mysteries, perhaps. In any event, the result was her slowness in communicating. But only to talk, not to sing. Because when Malvina sang she never stuttered. She sang without impediments, as if music injected a supreme power into her syllables.

Another doctor confirmed the stuttering as a minor, insignificant handicap. That's the word he used, "insignificant." It's a defect many babies are born with, even though their mothers aren't aware of it. He said it was possible to correct the condition through intensive therapy sessions and exercise and recommended a teacher who would improve Malvina's public speaking, with whom Malvina began private classes the following week that put her in a terrible mood. The therapist would force her to take a deep breath every time she began to stumble with a difficult word and made her think about the grammatical and syntactic structure of sentences. One of her requirements was that Malvina buy a thesaurus and read it every night before going to sleep. Whenever she would come across words that contained *t*'s and *r*'s, *p*'s and *r*'s, or *c*'s and *r*'s, she would have to memorize an alternative for each. This way, when speaking, she could avoid difficult words.

Malvina took speech classes for three or four years. Her mother forced her to, even if she hated them. She hated to talk, she hated to memorize new vocabulary. She only liked to converse with herself inward. When it was necessary to interact with others, she did it by playing music on a Yamaha piano her father had bought for her when she was a little girl and which she loved. As soon as the speech teacher would leave, Malvina would lock herself in the room to study melodies. An uncle had given her an instruction manual to help her learn how to move her fingers on the piano keys. Pieces by Bartok, Chopin, and Beethoven were her refuge.

Everything changed with the accident, a horrible experience that left her defeated. She could remember (how could she not) each and every detail of that fateful July morning when Esdras and her mother packed their suitcases and got into the car. They were going to take a ten-day vacation near a swimming pool in Tapabalazo. Her mother never liked to leave her daughter alone, regardless of her age. They were very close, and had been ever since her husband, Malvina's father, deserted them. But the young woman didn't like Tapabalazo because there were people with whom she had to be sociable. Esdras, whom she adored, tried to convince her to go, but it was to no avail. Malvina preferred to stay home. She felt without the urge to do anything. She had graduated from high school two weeks before and had been playing piano day and night ever since. Her Yamaha piano had been exchanged for a grand Steinway and Malvina dreamed of becoming a concert pianist.

The news of the accident was unbearable. Esdras's car had lost control, slid, and crashed into a brick wall. Her mother died instantly and Esdras barely made it to an ambulance. It was too much for her to handle. Malvina felt all the world was crashing down upon her. What would she do, alone and isolated, without anyone to keep her company? Her stuttering had resulted in an impenetrable introversion. She loved them. They were her only contact with the world. How would she go on living now? Alone, and no one's daughter. Brave and decisive, she eventually decided to discontinue the speech classes. If she stood out like she wanted to, it would be as a pianist. People would talk to her and she would reply with music . . . *her* music.

Strange physiological symptoms began to emerge. Malvina would wake up with an intense pain in her left ovary, as if someone had pulled on it while she was sleeping—an intermittent pain that made her cry. She went to a doctor for a check-up, but nothing was found. The pain stopped for a few days after she took some aspirins, but returned with the same intensity—as if someone was hurting her on the inside with a screwdriver.

Next, it wasn't her ovary but her left eardrum. Or her left leg, or her left lung . . . always on her left side. Malvina would scream and doubled up in tears. Esdras, who had been fond of Zen and oriental philosophy, had many books in his library that dealt with the mind/body duality. Malvina found one about the counterbalance of opposites. It was written by a Hindu shaman and it said if our fragile internal balance is broken, complications set in: troubling dreams, anxiety, lack of appetite, and pain in the left side of the body. Malvina, then, was sick, one side of her was heavier than the other. The solution, according to the author, consisted of a series of gymnastic exercises like crawling around in circles on all fours. Even though they looked comical, she still tried these and other exercises. She tried them all.

Exactly two years later the worst anatomical fracture occurred.

It either happened while she was walking to the bank or returning from the market, Malvina couldn't quite remember. Suddenly and without warning, she felt she was losing one of her hands, the left one. First she had it, then she didn't. The first thing she did was calm down and try not to pay too much attention to the entire incident. Fear could take possession of her, which was dangerous and could contribute to worsening her condition. Malvina took a deep breath. She didn't look around her because she thought people would be making fun of her. Her, a lonely young woman, staring at her hand and at other people in the middle of the sidewalk, how ridiculous! They might think she was still in high school, an immature and incomplete woman—a lunatic.

She walked a few blocks feeling nervous until she stopped at a corner, near a pharmacy. Then, once again, she took a deep breath. With her right hand she felt around for the hand that was missing. Malvina could see it. She pinched it but it didn't hurt. She caressed it. Her right hand had feeling, but the left didn't. She then concluded she had actually lost her left hand and what she was seeing was an optical illusion. The terror that came over her is indescribable. During that time she had been scheduled to give performances in the Haulcóyotl Auditorium and the Palace of Fine Arts. She would have to cancel them and live with the disgrace of being a one-handed pianist.

The left hand, *her* hand, returned a few days later. It was there, as much a part of her body as any other organ. Malvina cancelled only one of the concerts and performed the rest. But the agony of knowing that it could happen again didn't leave her in peace. What if she lost sense of her hand while playing Bach in public? How could she excuse herself knowing the hand would be there but not really? She was terrified. She would wake up early in the morning thinking she had an insufferable pain in her uterus and a few minutes later realize it was only her imagination. Or she would dream she was being cut vertically in half. Malvina and Malvina's ghost.

The feeling she had on that rainy October morning when she felt sure God (the smell of pine trees) was in the kitchen, was only the most recent evidence of those frightening pockets of anguish. And tomorrow, not tonight but tomorrow, she would get another identical feeling. She would wake up early in the morning and slowly put on her robe and slippers. With her nostrils wide open, she would walk down the stairs to the kitchen, longing to find, once and for all, the redeeming smell. But it would be a false alarm, of course. A smell of God? Malvina would see her own left hand on the kitchen table and start to cry uncontrollably. She would then lower her eyes, hoping the authentic hand, *her* hand, would be in its place. But no. She would swallow her saliva, sigh, and approach the table to touch her left hand with her right one. The entire incident would make her laugh . . . quite a bit, as her tears would dry on her cheeks. Only then would Malvina begin to give off a foul smell of pine t-t-trees.

TRANSLATED BY HARRY MORALES

TALIA IN HEAVEN

For Ofelia S.

The founding of the people [of Israel] affords a glimpse of its future destinies, but no more than a glimpse.

FRANZ ROSENZWEIG, *THE STAR OF REDEMPTION*

Un libro más es un libro menos.

JULIO CORTÁZAR, *LA OTRA ORILLA*

WAS SHE JUST A PATHETIC HALLUCINATION? YOU NEVER MET HER, LIFESHIT, admit it!

I wonder if one day I'll remember Talia's face. An illusory vision. Her story (like any other) could be told over and over. Who was Talia? She was eighteen times the bride of Adonai. I say it and I'll repeat it. . . . I've already said it a thousand times, to Dr. Yekutiel Me'eman. But he makes fun of me, he's unmerciful with my imagination.

"You didn't even know her, Lifeshit, admit it!" he grumbles.

"I know, but . . ."

I laugh like an idiot. I'm always on the verge of telling him (although he already knows it) that a perfect knowledge of anything is impossible, that intuition is enough. But I keep quiet, I don't know why. Dr. Me'eman listens only to my silence.

I was born in Paranagua. I can readily detect sarcasm. I know people in the city who live day after day with crises of identity, people who speak about anti-Semitism, about Judaism and other such things, people who have opted for violence. I know what I'm talking about, even if I do live in New York, even if today I'm close to G-d and far from Paranagua. I am a quiet man . . . but I'm not a fool. Paranagua isn't like other places; it's surreal, it's illogical, it's incoherent, it's like dynamite. If Kafka had been from Paranagua, he would have been a realist. Talia went there looking for the magical, the exotic; the idiosyncrasy of her land was of a different type. Paranaguans take advantage of the tourists. They suck them dry and leave them wriggling on their backs. It's a kind of revenge against their condition.

I was the one who invented Talia's mischief, her adventures. I invented her features, the color of her skin, her eyes, her smile, her anguish. I should be honest, I should confess: I read novels. I read them because poring over the dry religious tracts of the *Torah* day and night bores me. Talia touched me somehow, like a soft morning. It was during the Sabbath: I was hungry, desperately looking for a crust of rye bread, and I saw her; was she a spirit or a living thing? I don't know—now Talia is my character.

"Forget it, Lifeshit, and remember your duties, which already is too much for you," the doctor complained. He thinks I'm an imbecile, he and the rest of the Keter Malkuth congregation. According to my father, who died in 1956, I couldn't take care of myself, because I laugh like an idiot. It's true that I don't hear clearly and I see poorly. I wear thick glasses, my *payess* get tangled up around my nose, my black caftan is stained and I trip over my feet, watching the ground while I walk. I've got a bad left foot (a birth defect). Yes . . . it could very well be that I'm ugly . . . but, is it my fault? We have to look ever upwards, which is where everything is given to us and is taken away. My mind is fresh, always hungry for more. My father was thirty-three when he died, thirty-three, Christ's age. He left me in their care, with the prelate Nuchem and his cousin Rabbi Chaim Kopikis. They are in charge of all responsibilities and the community paperwork, and they're the ones who have me under observation . . . but they don't know (thank G-d) what I do with my time. Getting on the plane was frightening. Those monstrosities are fragile things . . . everyday you hear about another accident. I flew from Paranagua to Kennedy Airport right after sitting *shiva*. My father left us, saying, "Friends, cousins, New York is a dump, a circus tent full of chatterboxes and crazies. Protect my Lifeshit, my big boy. Make sure he's safe and protect his interests. I leave him to you. He's ignorant and humble, and if he isn't the messiah, he's not a heretic either, although he may look like one." Reb Kopikis and Nuchem received $50,000, and Dr. Me'eman is in charge of my education.

A few weeks ago the dining room almost burned up because I left the stove on. For that they took away my TV on Sunday night. Am I a failure? If I lose the sealed messages that Nuchem gives me to deliver to the Keter Malkuth members, the punishment is much worse: I'm locked in my room for three days—no jam, no milkshakes, no novels.

Yesterday I broke a candelabra and I dripped some incense on the carpet. My movements are brusque and rough.

"You're a fool, Lifeshit!" Dr. Me'eman says. "You walk around with a dazed look on your face and you've got nothing inside. Yet I love you, because you, unlike the others, you for one don't have a heart the size of an olive."

More important than the heart is the stomach. If we didn't eat jam and bread and soup, where would we get our energy? The stomach is where lies our intuition, as well as part of our intelligence.

I take my turn washing dishes or sweeping the synagogue, sweeping it just like Rabbi Yehuda Loew of Prague's golem, made of dust (Borges dedicated a lovely poem to him). Am I a golem? I sweep away the spiders who build invisible cities behind the furniture or in the Ark, or between the tassels of the curtains that guard the *Torah*. I sweep . . . I sweep and I think, I think and I recite things, I sweep and I recite things: *if* names are archetypes of things, in the letters of rose is the rose itself, and all of Lifeshit in the word *Lifeshit*. I tell myself while I'm sweeping, you have to begin Talia's story, because she herself asked you for it. But should I?

And, am I a golem? I could have held her, made her my wife. Now, which names did she mention to me? Were they people of Paranagua? Make something up, Lifeshit. Use your imagination. You're alone in the synagogue, nobody's watching you. The world exists so that people can imagine it. Talia . . . Stabans (or Stavans? How was it spelled and pronounced?) and his self-same . . . Igal Balkoff, Dr. Jekyll, Mr. Edward Hyde, and Dorian Gray. I'm hungry. Am I digressing? Think, Lifeshit, make something up. Very well, I now give you your own voice, Talia . . . *my* Talia.

―――

You have fornicated three times and you are exhausted.

It's May in Paranagua and you're with Stabans in the Narvarte apartment. You arrived here from Montreal three months ago. Where does the city hide its exoticism? It has, like all of them, big buildings, avenues, supermarkets, public transit, crime, and love. You had read its history in encyclopedias and guidebooks. Is what you found very different? You've come across a painfully poor and badly governed Paranagua. What is the difference between that and Canada's own peculiarities? The people here act more on their feelings and less by their reason. But you like the atmosphere, you feel good. You're far away from your mother, and that's something. You've come to find out who you are, why you're a Jew, and just what your destiny should be.

You want more than anything to have a baby! Your femininity has changed, you're no longer a girl. You're . . . how old? Twenty-seven? Twenty-eight? Perhaps you'll find a husband here. Would your mother be happy with a

Paranaguan son-in-law? Ha! For your mother (who was a refugee in these latitudes at the end of World War II), Paranagua signifies the dangerous, the unknown, the place where things are distorted. You wanted a setting where reality wasn't so scientific, where there would be space for chaos, where technology hadn't taken over everything. It lets you reflect on your future. If your mother has "dirty" memories of Paranagua, yours will be clean. You'll be the new beam of light, showing the way for the others. But you've come, also, to prove to your mother that life should be lived with risks, and that you're independent. You saved your own pennies; you don't want the money due you from your father's side of the family.

You'd never imagined that Stabans would engrave himself this way on your horizon. When you met them in the Montreal airport last year, did you hear what Ofelia told you about Ilan? You ignored her. Matchmakers belong to the past, especially the matchmaking mother. A young modern woman doesn't find a husband by playing the lottery.

They didn't even show you a picture of him. You didn't know if Ilan was handsome or ugly, sweet or nice. The "or" . . . handsome "or" ugly . . . the "or." This "or" that. You had a conversation with Stabans about that evil "or." You thought that dividing the world into two parts was amusing, didn't you? The history of humanity is the history of its divisions: whites "or" blacks, sex "or" intelligence, the aristocracy "or" the plebeians, the wise "or" the fools, free "or" enslaved, materialists "or" spiritualists. Make opinions, disagree, challenge, make room for categorization.

According to Kafka, there are those who deny misery by pointing toward the sun, and those who negate the sun by fixing instead on misery. Binominality is good, because paradise shouldn't be opposed by hell (the dogmatic Christian version), nor should reason oppose instinct (quite a worn-out equation). Sun against misery. The sun could be the sky, space, heat, light, or life—or simply the elevated, that which points to G-d, that which remains afar, untouchable. The contrary, misery, is darkness, the deathly, the beggarly. Misery is the absence of something . . . any absence, that of light, of heat or color. Misery is synonymous with cold and with pain.

You helped with this distinction, whose extreme includes those who divide the world into two—on one side those who divide the world in two and on the other side those who don't.

But Stabans denied these polarities. For him, oppositions were a reductionist act. The "or" is a lie, a farce. Why not black "and" white, hot "and" cold, brilliant "and" foolish? Why not support the various faces of the same object? You found this idea ingenious. We live in a civilization that glorifies unity: the unity of God (monotheism vs. idolatry), the mental unity of the individual (vs. schizophrenia), the unity of government (vs. anarchy). Why not opt for true versatility? Perhaps because we would disintegrate, and our ethics, wisdom, and social life would be flushed away.

It was an interesting talk.

You met Stabans at that dinner in Narvarte and then you saw each other again at the university. He played his role as professor with elegance. He'd arrive early, shoes shined, dressed in a wool sweater or a good suit, European tie and belt, silk socks, with a briefcase of Italian leather. He taught a course in medieval philosophy (Islam, Hebrew, and Christian) at the Universidad Autónoma de Paranagua.

You had heard about his classes; you entered his classroom and felt a singular pleasure, something between shame and enthusiasm. He reminded you of something in your past. Stabans flirted discreetly with his students, a touch of Humphrey Bogart. His personal file (a secretary gave it to you, after repeated pleas) read as follows: date of birth: 7/4/54; citizenship: Paranaguan; age: 34; height: 1.73 cm; weight: 77 kg; student ID number: 110-68-1966; current address: Motozincta 12; Colonia Narvarte; Paranagua, Fed. Dist., 216. Publications, titles. Collaborations on various national and international newspapers. His ancestors came from Bialystok, in eastern Poland. Jewish. Your mother wouldn't have believed it: a Jewish Paranaguan, neat, well-dressed, intelligent. What a dish! He spoke Yiddish, Hebrew, Ladino—what more could you ask for? He was tidy and organized, had a medium complexion, with brown eyes and blond hair.

The passion grew between you, and today you have fornicated three times.

°———,

It's hot out, the humid, suffocating heat that attacks cities every year.

A vigorous rain had fallen the day before and the radio has predicted more showers. It is now noon. After dozing a little, Stabans gets up. He's careful with the bandage on his stomach. He goes to the window, displaying his nudity. He opens it and leans out. There's a wind blowing. At last! A relief from the heat. Fat drops begin to splash on the pavement. It has begun to rain again. Half a block away, there's some sort of commotion. It's the traveling market, taking advantage of the clear sky to do some selling. They'll have to go now, with the rain starting. The vendors shout, advertising sweet oranges, parsley, tomatoes for salsa, where's the police, pewter frying pans, loofahs, brooms, look where you're going man, feather dusters, goddamn old hag gimme your can so I can play golf with your little dog's head, we got sackcloth, check it out, we got *pasilla* chiles, look and if you've looked then compare, if you've compared then make up your mind, come see our Cambrai lettuce, peppers, don't try to get in front of me, lady, fuck you ya old fart, corn from Guantánamo, aprons for the servants, hey let's push over that old cripple, hey Nureyev! bras and underwear for ladies, come on young man, let's go four-eyes hey lemme see your glasses, tires and tire-soled sandals for sale, tortillas, *huelly* for tea, *cola de rabo* and chicken mole, move it buddy you look like a smashed piece of spit. . . . Stabans hears it all. They're selling out the whole store. The racket is deafening and he imagines the horrible squawking going on for hours, perhaps forever. He looks up at the clouds. Definitely looks like rain—it won't clear up until early morning. Tomorrow is Saturday and luckily I don't have to go to school. He relaxes. He turns around, he looks for his watch on the bureau.

You roll over, trying to shake yourself awake. A breeze filters in through the window and makes the curtains dance; it's enough to wake you. You turn onto your back, and look at Stabans sitting on the chair.

He's opening a book, getting ready to read. What is it? Can you see the title? *High Art*. Mmm . . . you observe him carefully. You remember how you made love together. Utter passion. You remember the screams, the shuddering of so many ins and outs. While he made love to you he talked about masturbation.

"Masturbation is an illegitimate coitus with space. Space is one big vagina, a vast receptacle for semen. Cold, impotent demons stroll through the atmosphere, anxious to reproduce. If they do, they sire illegitimate children. These children are absent, invisible creatures who follow their progenitor around all his life. Then, at the final judgement, at the big showdown, they demand a duel with the biological children, the visible ones who were born through woman. Depending on who wins, the man goes to paradise, or to hell." Stavans then recommends that you masturbate. He recommends it because he lives life like a reclusive monk. He leaves home only to go to the university and spends the greater part of the day analyzing manuscripts. He doesn't involve himself with other people; he's very quiet. Judaism says there's no hell, that it doesn't exist. But, being a Christian, wouldn't it be more promising to go to hell? That's where all the souls of the intriguing people would be, the ones who had stirred things up in the world.

You say to him, "What's the difference between fornicating and masturbating?" "At least when you're screwing you can meet people," he answers. Stabans surprises himself and he looks at you. You both laugh. Discussing masturbation while making love, while sharing sex, is a joke, a contradiction.

Now Stavans is quiet. He's very unreceptive. Why has he loved you in this way? You're happy but you feel confused. Who is Stabans? You met him recently at the university. You don't really know what he wants from you. He picks up the newspaper that's below the bed. *Dr. Jekyll & Mr. Hyde* is playing at the Savoy Cinema. It's a 1920 film directed by Victor Fleming, starring Ingrid Bergman and Spencer Tracy. We could go, he says.

You don't answer. Why did he invite you to the movies? Something or other makes you think of Christ, who wanted to monopolize all the human suffering he could.

What kind of thinking is that?

You remember the folding screen that caused Stabans's wound on his stomach. Why hasn't he let you see the cut? Is he ashamed? After all, you've already proved you know how to take care of him, and that you'll give him affection.

You think: Stavans is strange, I have to be careful. There's something fascinating about him, and something else warning me against such easy seduction. He's a brave man, but where does his bravery lie? He's creative, he speaks beautifully—but there's a touch of something destructive in him, a bad mood somewhere in his spirit.

Why can't we see each other on weekends? Where does he hide himself? Is he seeing someone else?

You pull a pillow up like a backrest; you lean back; you continue to look at Stabans.

He turns the page and looks up. You get up off the bed.

"Where are you going?"

"To the toilet."

You leave the room, keeping your eyes down. You look at yourself in the mirror on the dressing table. Your hair's messy and you're pale. You wipe the sleep from your eyes and fix your smeared makeup .

A pattern of rain against the windows. You go to the toilet and the rain grows heavier. Suddenly, you hear an unearthly, powerful noise in the other room. You feel frightened. What is it? It was like the sound of boxes breaking, or bones, like a grave digger gathering corpses in the morgue. (Could it all be in your head? Do psychological sounds exist?) The sound continues. You let out a shout: Staaaaavaaaans . . . no answer. What's going on? Where is he? You finish up on the toilet, flush quickly, and run back to the bedroom. Did he hurt himself on the screen again? Once more the noise comes and now you're sure: it's the sound of bones breaking. Bones, someone's breaking bones. You look for your lover, for the professor. He's not in the room. You look in the kitchen, not there either. You're upset. Is the noise coming from the living room? You finally find him sitting in a chair, in the living room. But wait a minute! Stavans isn't Stabans. He's not wearing his pajamas. Did he have them on before? He's naked, he's disfigured, like he'd been hurt. There's a fuzzy down sprouting on his chest. It's growing in his armpits, on his thighs and on his forearms. His hair is disheveled; he has a bandanna tied around his head. He's trembling nervously. He's chain smoking. His sideburns are long; they reach down his face to his beard.

His complexion has changed. His face has a doubting, questioning, dangerous smile. How can this radical change be explained? It is, and it isn't Stavans. His bangs fall differently on his forehead. It's definitely not Stabans. Do you feel like throwing up? The wound on his stomach has been unbandaged. It is swollen, and suppurating a viscous liquid. It doesn't really look like a cut from glass, but rather the result of a gunshot.

What the hell is Stabans into? The person standing there reminds you of someone you saw leaving discreetly, after the dinner that Daniel and Ofelia had for you in February. You feel distinctly afraid.

"Talia—" Balkoff begins to say, like someone who knows the name but doesn't know who it belongs to. "How's it goin'?" You don't answer.

Your father told you this story. It's called "The Rabbi's Son" and was written in the first decades of the twentieth century, by Rabbi Nachman of Bratzlav, grandson of the Baal Shem-Tov: A young man has the same dream three times consecutively. The dream tells him to go to a village to speak with a certain rabbi. More for caprice than anything else, the young man's father impedes his trip, but then decides to accompany him. Along the way, fate causes a wheel of the cart to break. Father and son return dejectedly to the house. The father considers the accident a bad omen. The young man has the dream once more and, resigned, the father accompanies him. On the way they stop at an inn and tell their tale to someone there, who advises them not to go see this rabbi. The father convinces his son to give up the plan. Eventually the son dies. Years later the father runs into the same person from the inn, who says to him, sneering: "I prevented your son from going to the village because, in doing so, the Messiah would have come and redeemed the universe." The man was Satan.

Have you ever seen the devil? Does this world have enough strength to redeem itself? "The Rabbi's Son" stayed in your unconscious and has now come back to mind, because you've suspected something macabre in your love affair. How can you intelligibly explain the transformation you were witness to? You should (if the opportunity arises) tell Stabans the story. He's intelligent, he'll find a moral in it somewhere.

———

When did you first hear a description of Stabans? It was from his parents' own mouths, who were on a pleasure trip in Canada at the time.

It was the December before your trip to Paranagua. You were working as a receptionist at the airport branch of Budget Rent-a-Car. You had the night shift and waited on Daniel and Ofelia Stabans, along with their young est daughter, Liora.

It was the Tuesday before Christmas at 12:15. They were taking their winter vacation. They lived in Paranagua, in the Narvarte section. They had planned a road trip around your country's extensive land. They deserved it.

The last six months had been a series of unending work. Daniel was the one who looked most tired. His eyelids were irritated. He wanted to forget the animal feed store where he worked; he wanted to rest, he wanted to see the countryside, to be with nature. They had flown directly from Paranagua to Montreal. They were going to rent a car and see Ontario, Manitoba, and Alberta, stopping a week in the famous Rocky Mountains National Park. Actually, the trip was Liora's birthday present.

You waited on them kindly. You even made yourself their friend. You spoke to them of a chalet that your father (may he rest in peace) had in Alberta and offered them the use of it. It was a sign of kindness. They seemed like nice people.

A few hours later it came to you, while you were driving home. You had gone out of your way with them only to have another contact in Paranagua. Why did you need them, if you already had the Reznitsky's? You wanted to meet people, not to arrive and feel out of place. How could you have known that their destiny and yours had already been mysteriously joined together? How could you have imagined that fate would master you all and cause you grief? They wanted a Chrysler or Toyota, something with room, something functional with good mileage. You gave them a few choices and your help, in the end, saved them more than one setback. While they filled in the information and signed the papers, you talked to them about your plan to go stay in their capital city, Paranagua, and study in a local university there. It was to be an adventure. You wanted to take a vacation.

———

You told them that you'd saved money and you were counting on that amount to survive on. You added that you had some Paranaguan relatives whose last name was Reznitsky, and that you were going to stay with them.

"I don't know them," said Ofelia. You noticed her complaining about an aching in her bones. "Arthritis," she said. "It runs in the family. We Stabanses are of lukewarm, porous bones. One ancestor died of elephantiasis, and of the others, at least seventy percent suffer from arthritis."

"Is it painful?"

"Come on! The cold makes it worse. But there's a treatment in West Indian Perdridge that someone recommended to me; that's another reason why we came to Canada. They base the treatment on thermal springs. We arthritics, however, serve quite well as thermometers; we know when the temperature is going to go up or down."

You liked this link between bodies and the climate. "Your Spanish is fantastic," Daniel said. You replied, "My mother speaks it perfectly. She lived in the port of Veracruz for a couple of years and she made sure that Amnon (your brother) and I were multilingual since we were babies, and that we'd always be able to learn others easily."

"Liora's grandparents are from Eastern Europe, too." Stop. Silence. "What was your mother doing in Veracruz?" Ofelia asked.

"After surviving the Holocaust in Germany, she sailed to New York where her uncle, Harry Belfstein, was waiting for her, but when she got to the United States, she found that the immigration quota had already been filled and was closed. She had two choices: Camagüey or Veracruz. She chose the second and stayed in Paranagua for two years, working in a textile factory."

You wonder: Camagüey or Veracruz. And then you spoke together about Judaism. You gave them your diatribe (that you would later repeat to Igal Balkoff) about the ethereal, ahistorical, abstract existence of the Jew. You talked about Israel and the redemptive dream of creating a nation for Jews, but (you said) Zionism didn't attract you because it made the Jews too political, too material a people. You felt profoundly Jewish, but hadn't been able to reconcile your religion with your Canadian citizenship. You admitted that you were distressed by these kinds of doubts and that you were sure your stay in Paranagua would help you to organize your thoughts.

"The Reznitskys live in Tecamachalco," you said.

"Tecamachalco isn't in the center of town; it's on the periphery, did you know that? It's quite far from Narvarte," Daniel responded. "Public transportation is terrible. Tecamachalco's far from the university district, down in the southern end of the city. Having a car would really save you, Talia."

You asked if you should get an international driver's license. They replied that the North American one would do. You felt a lump in your throat. The trip was growing near.

You talked about other things and they finished signing the forms. You gave them the keys to the car and said goodbye brightly, wishing them a pleasant trip. Before they left, you asked if it were true that Paranagua was an exotic, mysterious place. They laughed from inside the car. "It probably will be for you. It all depends on the color glass you see it through." Ofelia said. They sped up the car. You turned and saw yourself reflected in a window. You looked at your smile, cheerful and pleasant. You saw the (yet small) wrinkles around your mouth and on your forehead. You had discovered them in the mirror that morning. Did other people see them too? Don't be such a silly child, you thought.

The Stabanses returned the car two weeks later. You had made a reservation, and that night (their last in Canada) you took them to a Portuguese restaurant and showed them the most picturesque little streets and neighborhoods of Montreal. You all drank wine from Amberes, then coffee, tasted delicious cakes and talked some more. When you asked them for their address, Ofelia (who was carrying something in her hands) described in detail her son Ilan. She told you he had his own apartment in Narvarte, that he lived quite close to them, really just a few blocks, that he was brilliant, single, and a professor at the university. They said nothing of his sometimes posing as Zuri Balkoff, of his disappearances, his exhortations against authority, or his tendencies toward violence. She wanted to sell you the whole package of goods, to persuade you. They loved the idea of having you there and would make a dinner in your honor.

You thanked them. The plan was to see each other in March. You would call them upon your arrival.

———

You landed. When destiny proposes, man disposes: You let days go by, perhaps a week, and then you called them. Ofelia's arthritis predicted a drastic atmospheric change for that day in March (the date of your invitation for a 7:00 P.M. dinner). It would be cold, rainy, and the sunset would end with heavy showers.

"Be sure to give yourself enough time. Public transportation will be a disaster." So many warnings . . . why do adults have that awful mania for giving advice? Could you have been able to visualize beforehand such an incredible amount of rain?

In the middle of the night before you went, strong, blustery winds and angry lightening brought great downpours over the city. The storm cleansed the air, made buildings shake, and cracked trunks of trees in Chapultepec Park. You should have been more careful, but no, your negligence obliged you to ignore the warnings: you arrived at Narvarte at 12:00 P.M. You were stuck for five hours in your Datsun like a ship in a bottle. You were buried in that tiny car like in a sarcophagus.

It was quite uncomfortable. Five hours. What did you do for so long? Turned on and off the radio, the motor, lights, and windshield wipers. You were restless, uneasy, embarrassed for getting there late.

Your internal monologues were endless. Mr. Policeman, we need help, we are trapped the water will drown us. What else was there to do? You opened a magazine, boring. You opened something else, a book, one by William Faulkner, *Light in August* (or is it *As I Lay Dying?*), that someone in the university had lent you: "Jewel and I come up from the field, following the path in single file. Although I am fifteen feet ahead of him, anyone watching us from the cotton house can see Jewel's frayed and broken. . . ." You closed the book.

You were depressed. Depression, synonymous with sinking . . . a sinking of the spirit. You felt suffocated, you felt disillusioned. Was this then a part of the national mysticism? You thought of writing a note to your mother but then thought better of it. You'd only end up quarreling. You leaned out the window (more like a porthole) and noticed that the level of water had risen. Continuing like this would surely overtake you. The water would sneak up into the car.

What was there up above you? Clouds like worms. How many magazines did you have? You tossed them aside. You felt ashamed by the whole situation.

Between Tecamachalco and Narvarte there are some eight kilometers. Paranagua, exotic city. What was going to happen? Not a millimeter of movement. You checked out the window again. An oceanic spectacle. Terrible, the sewer and drain system. Nineteenth-century Paris was a marvel compared to this. You thought of *Les Misérables* and of its chapters in the underground.

Trash floated by, as well as various mislaid objects. Were they bodies?

You saw firemen with suction hoses. You were hungry, you were in a bad mood. You'd have given your kingdom for a mortadella sandwich. You thought about the dinner Ofelia was preparing for you. Whaaat would she serrrrve?

There wasn't enough oxygen. It would be absurd to die like this, wouldn't it? The raindrops were like soap bubbles. You thought about the novels where, in a scene like this, the protagonist was left alone to confront his or her private being; it's always a stethoscope straight to their heart. They discover internal anxieties, epiphanies. You, you, you, could you be just a character in a novel, a novel, a noooovel? You slowly lost consciousness.

They got you out after forty minutes, purple, eyes swollen. They put an oxygen mask over your nose, and divers swam out in breast strokes to try to push the car.

Now you understood why the people referred to Paranagua as pure chaos, as a hole. Nothing like this had ever happened to you. You were thrown onto a stretcher . . . fifteen minutes . . . fifteen, or more? A policeman tried to steal your watch off your wrist. You struggled . . . you noticed that he smelled bad; with all your strength you bit him. Later you went to complain to the police chief. That accomplished nothing. You came to slowly and with difficulty. The rain finally stopped. The emergency rescue teams got the car going and this is how you arrived at the Stavanses' house—limping, dazed, without knowing how to look.

Liora opened the door. "What a drag! I've been in that damn Datsun for four hours."

"Daniel's stuck too, in the subway. The whole city's in an uproar. But now you can relax, girl; at least you made it. Do you want to take a shower? It would feel good."

Liora spoke in a soothing voice. Could you have suspected that an unhappy end awaited her? In our youth, death refuses to pass through our minds.

"Where is everyone? I want to say hello!"

"Hello!" A smile. "I'm Liora. You're Talia, that we know." Another smile. "Welcome!"

"Thanks."

She led you to the kitchen. The others were discussing the incredible rain (rain or cyclone?), and the perversity of nature. The television reported 65 dead, then 117, with 1,690 more missing. Could that be true? Were they exaggerating?

"Talia, we thought the worst," Ofelia said. "I'm still worrying about Daniel. What could have happened to him?"

Everyone was worried except Liora, who continued with her teasing smiles, imitating the commentator on the television (who was suffering from a stiff neck and had a red tie pulled tight in order to conceal it). She walked over to the fridge, hungry, complaining about the delay. "Papa will arrive," she said. "That we know. The question is, when?"

You should have called the Reznitskys to tell them that you were okay, but you stopped on seeing Ilan come down the stairs, and then, leaning gracefully against the threshold of the door, he saw you, too. He had his slippers on, and was wearing a pince-nez. His eyes were tired and bloodshot, he had definitely been reading. Had you imagined him like this? Strange thing, in the conversation that you had with the Stabans in Montreal, you never brought up an image of his face. You always did when someone gave you a spoken description of a person, no matter how spare: Why not this time? Ilan had a Saxony look, sort of Austrian in his facial expressions. He hadn't shaved and had a five o'clock shadow. There was a silence; you felt disoriented.

A noise in the lock. Daniel.

"I told you!" Liora gestured.

The father entered, greeting everyone. His nerves were frayed. He wanted to sit down. He had left the feed store at 6:50 P.M., five hours before.

"We thought the worst . . . ," Ofelia said.

"We thought you had . . . ," Liora imitated her.

"We always think the worst," Ilan added ironically. He turned to you and said something that you didn't understand. Did you like each other? No, he seemed vain to you, pedantic, conceited.

"The Red Cross, the United Nations' brigades, and other international organizations have sent food supplies, life boats, and medicine," he said.

Ofelia said that you had just gotten there as well.

"This was one of the worst days of my life," Daniel added.

"What happened?"

"It's not going well at the feed store. Shit, I'm fighting with Rómulo again."

Who was Rómulo? How many times had they fought before? Another silence. Ilan mentioned a medieval monk, Bahya ibn Paquda, for whom the earthly evils were merely a test of resistance that we as human must undertake. The comment seemed entirely too Christian to you and you said so. A conversation started up. You were testing each other.

Ofelia cut short the dialogue. She took tuna, sardine salad, and a carrot cake out of the refrigerator and set them out on the table. She asked Liora something and then took out plates, silverware, glasses, bread, lemonade, fruit jello, and avocado from the pantry. The television stayed on, the commentator stayed alarmed.

The telephone rang and was answered. You said (after being asked by Daniel) that you liked Paranagua and that you wanted to travel around, to Chichipotlán, Terezín, Monte Bello, and Tampico. You wanted to discover the secrets of the country.

Ilan smiled. Daniel went to wash his hands, same as Liora. They came back, everyone started to eat. You heard: Too bad the rain has come precisely the day that you came for dinner. We could have talked about other things.

All five quieted down to listen to the reports on the TV. During a commercial, Daniel started in with a little speech: In Paranagua, he said, the days are long and hard. Our political system is inefficient and decrepit. No hope left; Paranagua is a labyrinthine city where poverty reigns. It's a city that was never planned. The architecture is the product of an accumulation of buildings, people, and civilizations. We live like worms inside it. Food arrives dirty, decomposing. If we city dwellers suffer from something it's from a continuous bad stomach. In the national stomach is the key to our collective personality.

He was angry and you surprised. Why hadn't he talked like this in Montreal? They had wanted to attract you, like any other tourist, and you fell into their trap. Ilan (the apolitical Ilan that you met later when you were taken hostage) made fun, though furtively and with respect, of Daniel's "material" preoccupations.

The TV slipped into second place as Daniel continued: We have adjusted to what I call the "crippled" identity. The government will use this flood as a pretext to inspire piety—as they have done with earthquakes, plane crashes, and hurricanes. It will divert attention from more urgent issues: the agricultural depression, the gravity of the economic situation, the public debt, the price of tortillas, beans, and other staples. With this rainstorm, the State will have to reinforce its diplomatic strategy. They empty our stomachs, and fill our lungs with pollution. Who can still breathe these days? Who knows the taste of oxygen in this city? The government is rotting away. It's impossible to maintain this rickety image of Robin Hood toward the lower classes while the rich and the politicians of the country hoard capital.

Your lungs felt plugged up and you coughed. You thought of the flooding you had witnessed from your Datsun. What a surreal vision! In Canada, you told yourself, the people have more confidence in the State, they live more comfortably with themselves, they understand that they're urban people and that there are certain advantages and disadvantages that we must accept. But in Paranagua no, here everyone lives against everyone and meanwhile, G-d smiles. So much complaining, such a lack of willpower.

Daniel again, as he chews on a piece of bread: For example, the telephone. On every corner there are telephone booths that don't work. They belong to the State. Rather than investing in repairing them, they prefer to give away free calls to the user. This way, no one complains because no one pays. It's the same with electricity or with water: Paranagua's culture is one of self-absorption. First came the Spanish, who killed off the Aztecs and raped Indian women. Then they left—and invited the French, who substituted for the Spanish in the massacres and, the same, impregnated native women, only to leave afterwards. Today it's the United States here—and who will it be tomorrow? Knocking down Paranaguans is a French, Spanish, Belgian, Hungarian, and Jewish hobby. They dishonor us, laugh, and then leave. We Paranaguans are the fruit of these unhappy affiliations, both intrusive and violent. It's out of balance, the scheme of this culture and this identity—we're not who we are—and we pretend to be who we're not.

You felt a pain in your stomach and went to the bathroom to rinse out your mouth. They had warned you not to drink the water from the faucet, they had warned you back in Montreal to stay away from the spicy food, they had warned you that the people of this city were hypocrites, that they disguised themselves in order to seem friendly, complacent. So many warnings . . . was there truth in any of it? You said to yourself: I shouldn't have drunk the lemonade that Ofelia gave me, I shouldn't have eaten avocado.

Back to the table. What time was it by now? 1:25 A.M. You kept your eyes on Daniel.

In this instant Ilan, sitting on your other side, excused himself and left. Ofelia tried to keep him there; she shouted something after him but to no avail. You whispered to yourself, I'm not attracted to Ilan. I wouldn't want to see him again.

Liora watched the TV; it was a nightly music program.

Everyone finished dinner. "You're not thinking of going back to Tecamachalco now," Daniel said. Ofelia went out of the room and returned with some of Liora's freshly ironed clothes that she offered to you to sleep in. Why not stay? It was a logical suggestion. You accepted. You went into the living room. The sofabed had already been prepared.

Liora, Daniel, and Ofelia spoke again of the deluge, made some comment about the Jews, then said goodnight and went off to sleep.

Before she went, Ofelia told you, "Ilan shouldn't be long. I asked him to get the clothes from the washing machine up on the third floor before he went to his apartment. I'm sure he'll come back to say goodnight."

It was almost 3:00 A.M. You went into the bathroom and put on the pajamas. You came out and heard (again while you were looking in the mirror) a strange noise (it sounded like the bone-breaking one you would hear later in Stavans's apartment). It came from the kitchen. A couple of bottles fell to the floor and it startled you. You went to see what was going on.

Some lights went on and off. You saw a shadow. It was someone who looked like Stabans but had long hair and was wearing jeans. You felt afraid. Was it a thief? You wanted to scream, but didn't because the man closed a door behind him and disappeared in the blackness of the night.

You went back to the living room and got ready to go to sleep, feeling strange. Would you remember this tomorrow? You were very tired.

When you woke up the next morning, you called your relatives to tell them you were coming back; either they didn't answer or it was busy.

Ofelia appeared, asking what you wanted for breakfast. You couldn't bring yourself to beg out of it although you would have liked to. You ended up having what was a typical breakfast there: eggs with salsa, a plate of papaya, fresh orange juice, and sweet rolls.

You asked where the others were.

"They left early," she said nonchalantly. You yourself left a half hour later. You took the Datsun and, on the way back to Tecamachalco, saw that the city had dried out, the trash had been collected, the firemen were going about the daily routines, the drowned had been buried, blessed, and immortalized. No one remembered a thing. Memory, the key to our existence. You thought that perhaps in Paranagua events were easily forgotten.

Back at the Reznitsky's, you had an argument: they had been worried about you and had called the police. By coincidence, that same night your mother had called from Montreal. She wanted to see how you were, they told her you weren't there, she detected something strange going on and proceeded to call a thousand more times. You were angry, you shouted, you went up to your room and stayed there all morning, reading from the *Sefer ha-Malkuth.* Later on, you decided to go downtown. You assured yourself that the weather would stay nice, you put on make-up, brushed your hair, and just before you got into the car, the telephone rang.

"Hello?" You thought it would be your mother. "Hello, hello . . . ." Someone (a man?) was breathing on the other end of the receiver and didn't acquiesce to respond.

You hung up. It rang again. It was the same anonymous caller. You hung up and it happened three more times. You left the receiver off the hook. You asked the servant to hang it up in a few minutes and then you left the house.

You thought briefly of Daniel's rather long-winded speech last night: Paranagua as a hobby of the French, Spanish, Belgians, Hungarians, and Jews. Jews too? Jews tend toward the intellectual, not the sexual. Had you ever seen a macho Jew? You got into the car and started driving. You had trouble finding a parking space. You felt alone and in a cross mood.

You thought: hysterical . . . my mother is a hysterical Jew. Why didn't she just stop calling after a while? Was it impossible for her to give you your freedom? What would happen when you had your own child? Would she control it as she does you? Just get off your back, that's what she needed to do.

Did your stay in Paranagua (still) have any validity? You drank a cocktail in a downtown bar called Isla Negra (that you found by accident) and leaned your head down to see how the bubbles came up from the liquid.

❧════╍

The telephone calls continued.

A few days later you were feeling better, discovering a different type of reality there, a way to get close to things radically opposed to those with which you had been educated. You spoke with your mother and reassured her. She asked if you regretted the kind of education you had received in Canada.

No.

She told you that a young Jewish woman shouldn't stroll around by herself, without protection. "You must be more careful. You're too adventurous."

You made peace with the Reznitskys. They were good people, they were helping you out.

You spent your days at the university and seeing people. You were taking a course about migratory patterns and another one on St. Augustine. In the readings for the second course you had discovered some beginnings of anti-Semitism in the Church. You thought about it during your free time, thought about the conditions of the Jews as citizens embedded in nations that weren't their own and to which they didn't want to resign themselves.

You had more anonymous phone calls. In one of them the caller declared his name to be Igal Balkoff and then hung up.

He called again a few days later and began to talk to you about the class struggle in Paranagua. His voice sounded like Daniel Stabans. He swore he had seen you in the university. He followed you down the halls, he said, and watched you while you were sitting in the cafeteria.

It was a fact, his voice sounded familiar. It also sounded a little like your father's voice, a little more serious, maybe.

Was he crazy?

You began to feel pursued. You'd turn around as you walked to make sure there was no one behind you. You were suspicious, you were afraid to drive alone to Isla Negra.

The calls from this Balkoff guy kept coming. He'd talk about social violence, say he was in favor of it as long as it had an ideology behind it. He spoke of structural changes, of the poor, of the powerful elite.

It was during this time that you started taking one of Stabans's classes. You felt comfortable there. The professor was conceited but something in him attracted you. He winked at you when he saw you the first time and you struck up a friendship. You doubted that the friendship would go anywhere and it surprised you that it continued.

On morning an ungainly-looking guy, a hippie, came up to you outside the classroom and introduced himself. It was Igal Balkoff; he tried to kiss you.

You resisted. He said something about a historical figure and made a comment about Chapultepec Park, the Camarek section of town and the Aguaprieta National Palace, that was very close by. He was asking you, in his roundabout way, if you wanted to go there with him.

You said no.

He was so ugly! He declared that the Palace was a museum right now but would be a monument in the future.

You offended him by saying it was a lack of respect to call a woman on the telephone and not say anything when she answered. You begged him to stop doing it. You rudely said goodbye and left.

As you drove from the university toward Tecamachalco, you thought that Igal had the same complexion and appearance of that furtive, fleeting shadow, with its pyramidal head, that you saw in the Stabans's house that night. He had the same big nose, hmmmmm. . . . You remembered that that day some-one had read you Quevedo's sonnet about the man with the big nose.

Igal, could he be Jewish?

⌀═════╗

A week later.

Yesterday you had gone to the university but Stabans hadn't shown up. Not today either. Could something have happened to him?

You went downtown. In Isla Negra, you drank another (the same?) cocktail.

You had been studying for an exam and had come to the bar for a rest. You felt discouraged, you missed Stabans.

The position of your body over the bar (you had your head leaning on it), I don't know why, made you think of a certain way your mother sat while eating breakfast. Were you becoming more and more like her? She no longer called anxiously asking after you. Was she forgetting you? You thought again about the conversation after the dinner in Narvarte. It was right there; that was the instant that you began to see Paranagua as it really was: a swamp, a hole, urban brutality, craziness inhabiting the heart of civilization. You hadn't spoken with Ofelia or Daniel since then. They were sure to know, through Ilan, that the dinner had lit a fuse between the two of you, that the matchmaking prophecies of the mother had been fulfilled.

An old lady sitting next to you was reading the evening edition of *Excélsior*. You didn't see the headline at first. "Bank Robbery in Narvarte: $10,000,000 Stolen." You looked at the pictures. There, dressed in a green army jacket, was Igal Balkoff. . . . Next to him, another hooded man and one with a tie. Had they robbed the bank? Igal was hugging a machine gun and was bleeding from a wound somewhere near his stomach.

You thought about his stomach. You thought of his stomach as a symbol. You remembered that the hippie had spoken to you about an uprising and of a holdup. He and a friend were saving, he said; they had acquired a shipment of weapons and had to settle some accounts at a certain pier in Tampico in a few days.

You looked at the photo again. To know the criminal personally made you feel like an accomplice. You bought a copy of the paper and studied his face with more attention. Igal didn't have the air of a crook, but of a proud guerrilla fighter. He had a surprising resemblance to Stavans.

❧————❧

You felt an urgent necessity to speak with Ofelia. You wanted to ask her if she knew of an Igal Balkoff, if she could give you any information. The telephone was busy. Meanwhile, you followed the news on the radio.

The newscasters said that Igal and his partner, Dalton M., were fugitives. You read some in-depth editorials of a decided anti-Semitic tone. The rest of the group didn't matter very much or not at all; Igal Balkoff and his Hebrew heritage were the only target of the paper's attack. They laughed at the "assailing Jew" (parodying the concept of the wandering Jew). They gave a brief biography of him and commented that Igal belonged to a terrorist group with Maoist tendencies, and strong antigovernmental inclinations.

As last you reached the Stabanses on the phone. They were very frightened: Ilan had disappeared from his apartment, they didn't know his whereabouts. He had left some papers in the typewriter (articles for a periodical in New York City) but no note. The police were helping in the search.

You asked them if they knew Igal. A deathly silence. They invited you to come see them. You went and they received you (at first) in a friendly manner. They spoke of a certain incredible and improper behavior in their eldest son: he sometimes pretended to be someone else, to inhabit a different body. Igal Balkoff was his intimate friend or his ferocious enemy; he spoke of him with admiration or with scorn, depending on the occasion. He said that he was a brave man, courageous, pragmatic, or that he was a depraved coward. Other times he was his brother, his cousin, an old forgotten friend.

Some names came to your mind: Jekyll, Dorian Grey, Edward Hyde. Was Ilan a schizophrenic? You asked Ofelia for details, but she declined to give them. Her initial friendliness had turned into distance, silence. The courtesy the couple had shown you at the dinner back in March was gone. Although they smiled at you, they talked little, as if silence were more convenient. They gave you a coffee and it tasted cold to you (even though the cup was steaming). Strange: they didn't ask you a thing about your love for their son, nor inquired if his absence hurt you, as if the sweet family you had met at Budget Rent-a-Car in Montreal had simply melted. What hypocrisy! Had they deceived you once again? You said goodbye and left.

Who was Balkoff? You tried to remember his face, to recall his expressions. Nightmares began to pursue you. You dreamt of your mother in a tragic automobile accident or you saw her walking barefoot on icy, snow-covered plateaus, or in concentration camps, as Nazis tortured her . . . and you, Talia, appeared as a uniformed, indoctrinated member of the Gestapo. Your battle to separate your family from your personal discouragements and weaknesses also demanded a debate with your own ghosts. You have to understand, Mom, that my skin is our borderline. We are not one and the same person. You thought of the short novel by Carlos Fuentes, *Aura*, that Stabans had recommended to you, about the fantastic symbiosis between a mother and her daughter, one dead and one alive. You felt terror. . . . Who was he? What would happen tomorrow? What would you be doing in ten years? How would you perceive then the events of today?

Stabans returned to the university on Monday. He had a bandage that wrapped around his abdomen and he had to stop during his lecture to drink some water and rest. After class you went to inquire after his health; he told you he had been confined to bed with an illness, but it wasn't too bad, you didn't have to worry.

Had he been in an accident?

A small collision with a large window, a stupid act on his part, he told you. He had a folding screen in his apartment, with leaded stained glass, that separated the studio from the living room. He was putting away books on Saturday and tripped over a pile of volumes of the *Encyclopedia Britannica*. He fell and crashed into the screen, and a sharp piece of the glass embedded itself in his stomach. Did you suspect it to be a lie?

He turned down your offer to visit him at home. It bothered him to have other people in his house. Stabans, maybe Balkoff. You walked together down the hall and entered a classroom.

"You remind me of my father," you said, while you sat down on a chair. "He died three years ago. I miss the basement where he had his studio. He was a stamp and butterfly collector. He understood me better than anyone, the opposite of my mother."

Looking at the profile, or from the front, did he physically look like your father? The similarities were subtle: the line of his nose, the way his bangs fell, his sense of humor, the elegant way he dressed. It was raining outside. You opened an umbrella and the two of you left for Narvarte. In your Datsun, as you drove, as you spoke, you thought about *Aura* again. You repeated to yourself the names Jekyll, Dorian Grey, Edward Hyde, and added those of Consuelo, Aura and Felipe Montero. If you looked for them, would you be able to find these surnames in the *Sefer ha-Malkuth?* When you arrived at the Reznitsky's, you would open the book, and investigate in the index of names. Perhaps the key to the mystery that surrounded you would be revealed there.

⌁══════╮

You had the *Sefer ha-Malkuth* next to your bed. You treated it like a jewel; you read it, kept it clean, kept it hidden. The box it was in was a silver case that you polished every week until it shone like a mirror. You had looked for other copies on the shelves of bookstores or with antique dealers; you never found another one.

Who was the author? You didn't know and that's what attracted you about it: all books, you thought, should be anonymous. It mattered little or nothing at all who had written it. The important thing was that they existed, that they could be read and reread, analyzed. You believed in divine, in celestial inspiration. God was the true author of universal literature, God the channel of many inspired pens.

You read there of your future and your past: you didn't trust in the first, and you had to think carefully about the second. You trusted more in human global knowledge—and some of the divine. One day (you were sure) your own adventure would become part of that story.

The book lacked sequence, logic. Perhaps the copy you owned was an arbitrary sum total of pages of diverse origin (or maybe from just one origin), bound at random. Or it wasn't impossible that it was an incoherent translation, coarse and badly done, of, say, *Madame Bovary* or *Doctor Perplexorum*.

It had finely made sepia wooden covers with Gothic inscriptions in gold that glittered resplendently. It was slim and also thick, succinct and precise. You called it "The Book of Dreams" and you had bought it in Toronto, from a furrier who sold prayer books, booklets in Yiddish, and hermeneutics tracts.

You loved reading it out loud, poking around in the harmony of its punctuation and grammar. But your fascination focused itself, above all, in its quality for drawing out contradictions, anomalies, riddles, and trifles. Nothing more real, more authentically human.

You had spent weeks alone, reading, looking for sequence in the chaos. Stavans had disappeared again and reappeared. Had his injury, once again, been the motive for his withdrawal? You doubted it. The two of you began seeing each other, going out together. You went to the movies, to concerts. You were becoming a couple. You remembered when you had first realized you loved each other: you were at the university and went to get some papers. Stabans had to get his passport in order to travel abroad. He had to sign certificates, fill out forms, have his picture taken. Nothing bothered him more than photos and mirrors, because they reproduced the number of men, they multiplied them, and only G-d and sex had the right to such daring.

You were on your way with him to a photo studio but he suddenly changed his mind. You ended up in Isla Negra instead. You told him, just to see his reaction, about the time when you watched the bubbles in your drink and read in the newspaper about a neighbor who had robbed a house in Narvarte. You mentioned Balkoff; Stabans didn't flinch, he didn't know about it (that itself was suspect) and, without any more about it, you moved on to the next topic. Later he became nervous; you left Isla Negra for his apartment and when you got there, he fell on top of you and tore off your clothes in a burst. You felt him like a bull on top of you, and soon the pleasure of it possessed you.

You rocked back and forth, your breathing enveloped you, his arms took possession of your being. Afterward, you wanted to smoke. Cigarettes had never interested you but now an intestinal desire surged up in you. With a smile you said: "I need the smell of smoke." Suddenly Stabans got up; he pushed you away, rejected you. Your desire seemed to him irreverent, vulgar. What bothered him were the specters (he told you) that tobacco makes as it floats in the air, as it turns to smoke. He was allergic to that pestilence of burnt trees, to the toxic aroma, sick-making and nauseating. He stood up, went into the kitchen, and closed the door. You waited for him to come out. He took a long time. You put on a robe, went to the door, and put your ear to it. From inside you could hear a soft, rhyming singsong tone. After making love to you, Stabans was masturbating.

Your mother called again from Montreal. Whining. She wanted to know your plans. You were uninterested, you ignored her or tried to change the conversation. The particulars of your plans had become your tyrant. She wanted you to come home, there was no reason for you to be in Paranagua. In your reflections you understood that the improvement or worsening of your relationship with her represented the similar improvement or worsening of your self-esteem. By design, you, Talia, were her extension, a traced copy, a repetition of her, and Stabans (you felt it more everyday) was the copy of your late father. Perhaps the history of human romance was a sequence of infinite repetitions, every one of them spinning around a pristine ideal love, a generative and Edenic romance.

You wanted to stay in Paranagua because it was allowing you to reflect on the reaches of your being, of the other and of G-d.

Does G-d have an individual relationship, one on one, with every individual? Your thoughts about eternity, about human psychology, about the metabolism of objects, grew deeper, and sometimes you felt, not in the sphere of intelligence but in that of sensation, that G-d scorned you, that G-d wanted to test you, to play, to have fun with you. You thought of the image of the cross and then, again, of Christ.

One of the last telephone calls you had with your melodramatic mother went as follows:

You: As I was in the downtown train, I heard a nice saying today.

Mom: You shouldn't be on the subway. It's dangerous!

You: Mom, the Paranaguan subway is clean and safe.

Mom: I didn't mean . . . You have your own car; why take the subway?

You: I don't like being a foreigner. You know that, Mom.

Mom: Yes, I know.

You: Anyway, I wasn't paying much attention to what was going on around me. Then this bum, an old guy who smelled bad, came up to me and he said: *I don't care if it rains or freezes, 'long as I have my plastic Jesus. . . .* Can you believe it, Mom? In English. An Hispanic bum speaking English. . . .

Mom: I've read that somewhere.

You: You have? Where?

Mom: Yes. In a short story or something. I think it was Carlos Fuentes.

You: Since when do you read his books?

Mom: Since you left. I'm also getting interested in . . .

You: Really? Why do you always find something wrong in what I say?

Mom: What did I do now, Talia?

You: You know what I'm talking about, Mom.

Mom: No I don't.

You: Yes, you do.

Mom: Talia, if you're having problems . . .

You: Leave me alone.

Mom: Listen to me.

You: No. Leave me alone. Didn't you hear what I said? I need to be alone.

Mom: You *are* alone, aren't you?

You: Yes and no. You're there, always after me.

Mom: What are you talking about, Talia?

You bit on a pencil while you talked, and crumpled up a sheet of paper, tore up an orange peel, drew funny faces in a book, or retouched newspaper photos with glasses and moustaches.

Mom: Why are you so happy there, dear? You could be happy here, too.

You: Leave me alone.

Mom: Who is he?

You: Who is who?

Mom: He . . .

You: I don't know what you're talking about.

Mom: Mrs. Reznitsky told me you have a boyfriend.

You: She did?

Mom: Who is he?

You: Stop questioning me, please.

Mom: I want to know his name.

You: Stabans.

Mom: Stavans?

You: Not Stavans, Stabans, with a "b" as in boy.

Mom: "B" as in *burro*. Does he have a career, or what?

You: It's none of your business.

Mom: I guess he isn't Jewish.

You: Go on guessing. I'm in love and that's what counts.

You hung up and felt like an idiot. You were defending a ghost. Stabans had disappeared again. Incredible; was that the third or fourth time? You had premonitions about Balkoff; you dreamed he had made you pregnant, he had you gagged you in a torture chamber, he had raped you arduously in the back seat of the Datsun. You wanted to be a mother, didn't you? What price were you willing to pay? Weeks later, Stabans returned, and with him came his silences. You were furious, you didn't want to see him, you understood less and less and even though you got back together, he never told you why he had left.

It was here, a rainy day in May, with the gibberish of the marketplace, that Stabans transformed into Balkoff.

———

A paragraph (in present indicative) included in the *Sefer ha-Malkuth* describes Stavans's transformation in the following way: "A pattern of rain against the windows. You go to the toilet and the rain grows heavier. Suddenly, you hear an unearthly, powerful noise in the other room. You feel frightened. What is it? It was like the sound of boxes breaking, or bones, like a grave digger gathering corpses in the morgue. (Could it all be in your head? Do psychological sounds exist?) The sound continues. You let out a shout: Staaaaavaaaans. . . . No answer. What's going on? Where is he? You finish up on the toilet, flush quickly, and run back to the bedroom. Did he hurt himself on the screen again? Once more the noise comes and now you're sure: it's the sound of bones breaking. Bones, someone's breaking bones. You look for your lover, for the professor. He's not in the room. You look in the kitchen, not there either. You're upset. Is the noise coming from the living room? You finally find him sitting in a chair, in the living room. But wait a minute! Stavans isn't Stavans. He's not wearing his pajamas. Did he have them on before? He's naked, he's disfigured, he's been hurt. There's a fuzzy down sprouting on his chest. It's growing in his armpits, on his thighs, and on his forearms. His hair is disheveled; he has a bandanna tied around his head. He's trembling nervously. He's chain smoking. His sideburns are long; they reach down his face to his beard."

His complexion has changed. His face has a doubting, questioning, dangerous smile. How can this radical change be explained? It is, and it isn't

Stavans. His bangs fall differently on his forehead. It's definitely not Stabans. Do you feel like throwing up? The wound on his stomach has been unbandaged. It is swollen, and suppurating a viscous liquid. It doesn't really look like a cut from glass, but rather the result of a gunshot.

What the hell is Stabans into? The person standing there reminds you of someone you saw leaving discreetly, after the dinner that Daniel and Ofelia had for you in February. You feel distinctly afraid.

"Talia—" Balkoff begins to say, like someone who knows the name but doesn't know who it belongs to. "How's it goin'?" You don't answer.

And the *Sefer ha-Malkuth* adds (now in past indicative): You offered Stabans a cigarette and he started to shake. He was enraged. It was Igal Balkoff who asked: "What's going on?" A change of owners, a change of voices. It was the first time that you had seen Igal since the robbery. You were shocked, you wanted to hit . . to hit him . . . to hit both of them . . . but you didn't. You did punch your fist into the wall and then pack your suitcase. The whole thing was a sea of uncertainty. Should you cry? How could you explain something that was not of this world? Not a piece of glass; it was a gunshot. How foolish you had been, Talia!

When you came out of the bedroom, you were alone in the apartment. You didn't know where to go or whom to ask for help. You were horrified. You went back to the Reznitsky's (always your refuge in time of war). Hours went by, then days. Soon the kidnapping happened. That day you had decided to go out for a walk; you wanted to buy some magazines and if you felt like it, you'd go grocery shopping. You had just a few pesos.

You had a headache and had taken two aspirins. It was two o'clock in the afternoon. As you put the key into the door of the Datsun, you saw a green Volkswagen driving toward you. The street you were on in Tecamachalco was not a busy one; it could have been a neighbor but the car was going suspiciously slow. The green color made you think (again) about Aura, where the people look green and always dress in that color.

The Volkswagen had a dent in a section of the trunk and its tires squeaked against the bumper. You turned around. You thought you saw two people behind the old dusty windshield. Then you realized that someone had put gum in the lock of the Datsun. There was no way to open it. A man got out of the Volkswagon and threw himself on you. He pressed his lips against yours and then placed a piece of cotton wet with chloroform on your mouth. You kicked, you spit, you bit. Your money fell to the ground; no one picked it up. They threw you into the back seat. You slept, and a while later a man violently opened your legs, pushed, took you. You screamed (or you think you did). You felt his semen enter you, going up into your body, echoing inside.

⸻

Every night of love is different. No two are alike.

You had heard this anecdote from Stabans's lips. When? You don't remember. A respectful Jewish man, a preserver of G-d's honor, went to see the Rabbi Eleazar. He was planning to build his new house and wanted advice. "What do you say, Rabbi," he asked him, "how should I build the structure that tomorrow will be my home?" Rabbi Eleazar opened the Talmud. "Rabbi Ahaz ben Hanna," he answered, "suggests 14 piles of cut wood; 315 *maravedis* worth of baked brick; tacks; nails; a mallet and a ladder." The pious man followed the instructions carefully and built his home. He looked at it, completed, and wanted to bless it, so he nailed an amulet on the front doorpost. As he did, the building fell to the ground. He went back to the rabbi and asked him again to read, one by one, the instructions. The rabbi not only did, but he went back to the site with him, and made sure the tools and materials were correct. While he was building his house for the second time, the Jew read books of the learned.

Nothing was missing and after two days, the house was once again raised. Happy, the pious man decided again to affix the amulet, as should be done on every faithful house. Once again, the house crumbled to the ground. The man went back to Rabbi Eleazar to ask him what had gone wrong. Perplexed, the rabbi read one more passage in the Talmud and then answered: "Rashi the Talmudic scholar poses the same question."

What is it about amulets, that they sometimes serve to embitter us? Our faith in them turns us on our heads. They are fetishes, pagan, tribal objects; they demonstrate that monotheism and idolatry have not yet been fully separated. To trust, to believe, to have faith: these are not simple acts. Your parents had been believers, during the years of their marriage they had followed the traditional rules: rest on Saturdays, fulfill the liturgical rites, and they followed, to the letter, the obligations of the High Holidays. But they were not happy. As a girl, you had felt their religiosity to be outlandish behavior, without sense, and you had a special disdain for amulets. There was one, covered in gold and with a relief of two tigers and a deer, on the doorway of your family home.

Believers (like them) trusted in happiness but never achieved it because they live supersaturated by G-d. You knew it: happiness is to be found on the edges of religion and of G-d; it is ephemeral, brief, and has no relationship with heaven.

Your nights of love with Stabans were flashes of a passing happiness, religious acts, rituals of adoration, liturgical works, amulets of a hedonistic G-d.

⸙

Nightmare. The rhythm of breathing lengthens inhalation, freezes it; you recite during moments of insomnia: "This torment of love / that is in my heart, / I know I feel it / and not why." Archaic memories, collective memory. "This colored counterfeit that thou beholdest, / is, in fallacious syllogisms of color, / nought but a cunning dupery of sense. . . . Is an empty artifice of care . . . / a foolish sorry labor lost, / a conquest doomed to perish and, well taken, is corpse and dust, shadow and nothingness." Where did you hear those verses? This shaking flour? Pyramidal. Who's speaking? Insomnia. Where am I? 1391, a year of pogroms against the Jews in Spain.

Heavy, intense rains, rich harvests. St. Augustine: Spit on them . . . denigrate them . . . but don't kill them! They are historic proof of our lord Jesus Christ. Absurdities, anti-Semitic arguments and many wounds that day, a tally of forty deaths. There are those who predict the arrival of the messiah. Perhaps you have him there in your womb! G-d in the heavens: "Where is your wisdom?/ exalted, implacable, ultimate,/ from your throne you watch over the feats. . . ." Talia imagines being inside an onion two or three centimeters around; its concentric layers envelop her, allowing her to see everything from a privileged perspective from any angle she sees the gray hall in Veracruz where her mother lost her virginity with a Norwegian sailor she sees Walter Benjamin and Oscar Wilde she sees the survivors of the Holocaust she sees Mendele Mokher Sforim and Boris Vian she sees the sun and sees poverty she sees a Kabbalist, Isaac Luria, who is green, she observes on a desk the *Sefer ha-Malkuth* she looks at Stavans and at Miguel de Cervantes returning from somewhere in Argel the onion begins to rise defying gravity dreams insomnia cold the cold always complicates things must put on a sweater it isn't easy to have faith maybe it's because the shirt is sticking to the wool of the sweater but it's so difficult to get her arms through little by little she advances finally one finger peeks out with one tug the sleeve is pulled down and she looks at her hand as if it weren't hers are those really her fingers? where are you, Juana de Asbaje? she pokes her head into the sweater and her eyelashes snag on the uncomfortable wool the wool is wrapping itself around her face where is her back then? even though her hand touches it she couldn't swear that it's her face it looks like the sweater has bunched up shame where is the other sleeve? where are her cheeks? where are you, Talia? You recite: "Let those who, with green glasses spectacled, / see all things sicklied o'er with their desire, / questing for thy light pursue thy shadow: / but I, more mindful of my destiny, / imprison my two eyes in my two hands / and see no other thing that it I touch."

Your respiratory rhythm accelerates.

You woke up. You were in a freezing cold cell. You heard outside the wheeze of trumpets and the pedaling of a bicycle. You were sweating; you had had a terrible nightmare: you had wanted to put on a sweater while you were sleeping. The cell was dark, inhospitable. You tried to pull yourself together.

It was nighttime. A window let in the light of the moon, feeble and sad. You leaned back against one wall and saw that it was made of wood; it had been fashioned hastily and was painted white. You tried to make yourself believe that you were in a prison. You stretched your legs and it almost made you faint. You wanted to pee.

There was a locked door to your left. You felt strong, sharp pains on your right side; you turned and saw next to you, open at random, the *Sefer ha-Malkuth*. You began to read, happily. There was a detailed description of the confused dream you had had, of the sweater you had put on.

You heard steps; a door groaned. A hooded figure arrived and slipped you a tray with soup. It was cold. You wanted to tell the person something but he (or she) disappeared too quickly. The presence came two or three times in the course of five hours. The last time, when you tried to talk to it, he or she ignored you.

You shouted with desperation and your voice must have been heard kilometers away. You calmed down. You were hungry and voraciously ate up that vile brew. You felt dizzy again and vomited. Later you slept.

You opened your eyes. Stabans was standing there, looking at you. Was it he or wasn't it? He was whispering something; you didn't understand him.

" . . . in May. The weather in Paranagua is a drag. The mutations. It was difficult to know. *Dr. Jekyll & Mr. Hyde* by Victor Fleming. . . . Fantastic. One goes to the Savoy Cinema. . . . We lived our life without thinking about those who have completed the same ceremony, choosing the same place and the same time, dressed the same or telephoning to reserve the eleventh or the fifth row in a restaurant or at a concert. The earth should belong to no one. Perhaps we attempted some feeble words to excuse us for arriving late. It's difficult to know, above the urban mundane noise, that we were so many, those who loved you, Talia, that we were a club of admirers. . . ."

"Stavans?"

"What?"

"Where have you been?"

Your conversation sounded empty, taken from a Mexican melodrama from the sixties. Stabans went on: "In the book, the identity of Jekyll and of Hyde is a surprise; the author saves it for the end of the ninth chapter. The allegorical tale pretends all along to be a detective story—no reader could guess that Hyde and Jekyll are the same person. A cinch to turn it into a movie."

"I'm afraid," you replied.

"The munitions are stored in a warehouse. Balkoff was planning to rob a supermarket in the Romances neighborhood, but I convinced him to wait until tomorrow. There's not much time left; I should hand over the body soon. You'll see, I suppose, tomorrow at 3:00 p.m. Anyway, he'll use you as a scapegoat. Do you remember the story of Patty Hearst, the daughter of a rich family who was kidnapped by a revolutionary group in North America and later adopted the ideology of her kidnappers? They'll try to do the same with you."

"I curse the very moment I arrived in Paranagua."

"They are working for a cause and won't delay the project. They're raising money. . . . Deep down they're good people, filled with longing. They want to change the world and believe that violence is the path that will let them reach this truth. Revolutions are social exclamations, events that mark the culmination of an age, and it's possible, Talia, that we are living, without knowing it, the twilight of an epoch."

"They'll get him just for being a Jew. It's been done before."

"Of course."

"And you, Ilan . . . they've taken advantage of me. One of them raped me in the Volkswagen."

"You dreamed that, Talia."

"You're crazy. He robs banks, too, he's a bandit. Keep me out of his atrocities."

"His acts are mine. I rob banks and supermarkets. Balkoff trusts that this will be a victory to strengthen the spirit. The rest of the boys are enthusiastic. So far there are no casualties, thanks to G-d and to courage."

You let a few moments go by. Then you said, "Where is Igal? It's useless to prolong this stupid change of personalities . . ." Your words were cut off by the sudden outward change of the person speaking to you. A cigarette appeared, that certain expression of Humphrey Bogart disappeared, and you saw a bandanna. A minute later Balkoff was gagging you and two days later, when you came to, you realized that that disgraceful gag, drooled on, pulled tight, had closed your mouth forever.

⌐————ꝋ

You found yourself in a Chrysler. You were moving slowly on a highway full of potholes. Your eyes were bandaged. "I'm thirsty," you said.

"Shut up," someone answered.

You didn't recognized the voice. The car stopped. Silence. They took the cloth off your eyes. You were in a parking lot; it was afternoon. It had just rained and the air was humid. The hooded one next to you pointed a machine gun at you and, without anything more, wrenched you up out of the seat. "Let's go into the woods first," the driver said, who had a silk stocking over his head to hide his features.

The motor was turned on again. A few minutes later you were driving into the underbrush. "Stop here," the one in the back said.

"Where is Igal?" you asked. "I want to speak to Igal Balkoff."

Nobody responded. They got you out of the car. They pointed the gun at you again.

"Hold the gun," you were told. You didn't know what to do. You embraced the object fearfully with your left hand and put your index finger on the trigger. You were confused. The grass was wet and the sound of the wind as it hit the dead leaves made you nervous. They took a picture of you. The hooded one climbed on top of you.

When they had parked the car again, the driver turned to you. "You're going to drive like a queen, you understand?" he said to you.

It was Igal's voice.

"I want to go to the Reznitsky's," you said.

"Shut up. You're going to wait in the car. When we get back you're going to drive up Avenida Vasconcelos and just keep going, until we're far, far away."

"I don't know what you're talking about," you went on, but Balkoff wasn't listening. He drove the Chrysler until he arrived at a supermarket. It was on the side of the highway. The cars in front, against the facade, the rays of the sun, the shadows on the sidewalk, made you think it must be around 5:00 P.M.

"Get behind the wheel and wait there. If you make a mistake, you fucking Canadian, you can forget about your pretty neck." The two hooded men got out of the car, each with a case, and walked toward the supermarket. You watched them go. Now, you thought, now is my chance to run. You tried to turn on the motor at the same time as you floored the accelerator.

Your right leg was numb. Again you felt dizzy and your stomach growled. You hadn't eaten anything solid in days. I'm sick, you told yourself. The taste of vomit came to you and your heart began to pound. You wanted to escape but you weren't strong enough. You closed your eyes. Heaven makes mistakes, you thought, heaven plays jokes. I have come to the fatal cross-roads. Had I approached my discovery with a more noble spirit, had I risked the experiment while under the shield of generous or pious aspirations, all would have been otherwise—and from these agonies of death and birth I would have come forth an angel. How many souls are there in all the cosmos? One thousand, ten thousand, each one created by the All Powerful on the last day of creation . . . those who will die at age seven, at thirty-five or at eighty, those who will sin, those who will suffer from a physical deformity. Pomponious (follower of Plotinus) proclaimed that there existed in heaven a waiting chamber (in a place between the antepenultimate and the penultimate celestial sphere), where every spirit (divine puffs of wind, according to the Bible) waits its turn to descend to the material world. The descent is not a punishment, but rather a reward. To cultivate oneself, to perfect oneself and find happiness—those are the prizes offered. The mystery of the cosmos is revealed, born of the breast of hell. Boom! Boom! Magnificent, splendorous. The stellar gate opens its doors and the spirits line up, ready for their pilgrimage. The celestial exit is watched over by guards, shining hulks like St. Enoch. These guards cordially bid farewell to those on their way down, but sometimes they err, sometimes they let two souls go into one body. Is that the explanation for the cohabitation of Stabans and Balkoff? What happens is, there is the risk (one time in a millennium, perhaps) that an error be committed: two souls penetrate one portion of matter. But something is wrong . . . something is mixed up, something juxtaposed in the personalities of your lover(s), erasing the edges. Where does Stabans end and Igal begin?

You heard a shot. Igal and the other one (Dalton M.) came toward the Chrysler carrying a bag. Now Talia, hurry, turn on the motor! You tried, but your leg was still numb. They arrived at the car and got in. "Let's go," Balkoff said.

"I can't."

Without waiting for further explanation, Balkoff slapped you in the face.

⸻

On the highway now, at full speed.

They put on and then took off (out of compassion) a scarf from over your eyes. You saw mountains, unfinished buildings, cattle, fragile huts, corn and bean fields, and mules surrounded by wolfish dogs that barked or chewed or sniffed at shit on the ground.

There were mule drivers loping along, or swatting at cattle, or curled up near the bonfires. It was a floating rural population, who worked in Paranaguan factories earning minimum wage. Poverty, you saw a poverty you had never seen before. You noticed scattered towns, solitary, sorrowful. Farther away you could see the smog and hear the rumblings of the city.

The three outlaws (counting you) in the Chrysler went through remote outlying areas, lost villages, belts of misery.

Balkoff was arguing. "You shouldn't have shot them, Dalton. That could have meant the end of our project, not to mention our lives. How many police did you hit?"

"There were two on the ground. One with a hole in his cheek and another bleeding from his arm."

Silence. "How much money did we get?"

"Three million pesos."

"More, I think."

"I doubt it."

"That would make eleven million, seven hundred fifty thousand pesos altogether. How much would they give us for the girl, Dalton?"

"Enough."

"Do you think Tuerto would want to trade the guns?"

"I hope so. The boys are worried. The ones from León Shestowo are dying to help us out. We don't really need those fairies. How much should we offer them?"

"Five hundred thousand a head."

Balkoff turned to talk to you. "Sorry about hitting you. It's just that you don't understand anything about politics, Talia. You're hopeless."

"Fuck you," you answered, adjusting your vocabulary to the reality that surrounded you.

"What?"

"Fuck you. I couldn't give a shit about your goddamn country, Igal. You're no revolutionaries; you're delinquents."

Silence in the Chrysler. Was it a stolen car, too?

Then: "Dalton, I don't see or hear any police cars. It's strange that they aren't following us. Let's go to Camarek."

They went around and around; they circled blocks, they avoided some police cars parked up on the sidewalk, they arrived at the headquarters, they accelerated once more, they drove around, they sauntered, wandered; they floated. They drove into Chapultepec Park and you saw areas you recognized. It was a three-hour trip altogether. You saw a sign in the peeling doorway: it said Donceles #815, formerly #69. You all went in furtively, trying not to look suspicious. You limped on your left foot (it had fallen asleep). Dalton immediately locked you up in the cell.

———

Your Paranaguan adventure, no doubt about it, was ending up an enormous failure. You were depressed, lost, and you stank. You took refuge in bad moods and a bad attitude. You did not respond to them when they called you; you bawled out the young soldiers, with their flattops and naive stares, who served you soup. You grumbled, you growled, you whined.

Your disgrace was confirmed when they obliged you, pressing the barrel of a pistol against your temple, to write the following missive, with a ball-point pen on a yellowed, wrinkled piece of paper that was burned on one edge and stained with salsa: "Dear Reznitskys: I need help. My captors demand ten million pesos as ransom. Give it to them! Talk to my mother. She has money. The conditions of my cell are worse than deplorable: there are rats, cockroaches and the air is damp. They promise to use the money for laudable objectives. They will deliver me 'safe and sound' when they see the money. Yours, T.K."

A lie: if the conditions weren't Edenic, they also weren't miserable. No damp air, not one cockroach, and not cold at all. They had given you a sweater and two blankets. Even though it was dark and confusing, you were fairly comfortable, and this you had recognize for what it was; comfort hadn't been a frequent sensation for you in the last few years.

The next day they brought you another dish of food. It disgusted you. When you were hungry, they didn't bring you anything, but once you had lost your appetite, they gave you things that looked like feces. Later, Igal came. His beard had bulked him up. He looked like a picture-perfect revolutionary. He brought you magazines and newspapers. He sat down and showed you the headline of *Excélsior*, dated the beginning of July. You saw a photograph of yourself, holding a machine gun. Trouble! You were dazed, aghast. You spit at your captor, you bit him, scratched him, you pulled his hair and slapped him. Stabans had been right; they were using you to further their own aims. When you had calmed down, you read through cloudy eyes: "Delinquents Rob Supermarket in Nahualtoro with Stolen Car, Foreign Woman Involved." Shit. *I don't care if it rains or freezes. . . .* I want to get out of here. I belong to another reality. If you consider it a legitimate act to kill policemen in order to bring about better conditions for your country, go ahead. But don't mix me up in your dirty waters. I'm from another planet. From another planet.

You liked that description: Paranagua and Canada were, effectively, two planets where justice, idiosyncrasy, and human values were defined by opposing principles.

You exploded and the frenzy was good for you; it aided, in advance, your later reclusion, the hours of recollection, observing fictitious stars in an imaginary firmament, in your time away from the world. You lost your barriers. What was happening to you inside, in your heart, and what was outside? You looked at the newspaper, at Balkoff, trunks, packages of Paranagua, you heard sounds of cadets, the doorbell, a blender, a hood, three million pesos, Tuerto called, if he wanted to change the signal for the apartment on Donceles, the red and green Paranaguan flag, you heard the sound of cadets, the doorbell, a blender, pouch, three million, they talked about Tuerto, if he wanted to trade the guns, a thousand boxes of contraband liquor for the rest of the shipment and he'll wait for us at the corner of the high school, you're crazy, who's crazy, León Shestowo, the asshole, who is, the doorbell again, five hundred thousand pesos a head, you have to be an idiot to see things that way, asshole, shit-for-brains, shit, I don't care if it rains or freezes. I want to get out of here. I belong to another reality. If you consider it a legitimate act to kill policemen in order to bring about better conditions to your country, go ahead. But don't mix me up in your dirty waters. I'm from another planet, from another planet. You were on the front page of *Excélsior*. Did you feel disappointed? Your son or daughter, in the future, would title the story: *My Mother was a Criminal;* he or she would call you *ladrona*, thief, son of a bitch. You wanted, instead of a child, that a blind angel come forth from your belly, an angel that didn't distinguish between good and evil, that confused reality with fantasy, like Homer or Borges or Maharal of Prague's Golem. You looked at the photo a hundred thousand times. Yes, it was you, it was Talia, a famous Talia. You tore out the page, you kept the photo, you put it between the pages of the *Sefer ha-Malkuth* (or had it been there all along?). You were tired. You threw yourself down on the mattress and you heard a spring pop. Was Balkoff still nearby?

Did G-d have some purpose in having you kidnapped? It must be so; it couldn't be for nothing. You were a slave, the screw in an incomprehensible mechanism, a weak antenna, without projection, communicating an indecipherable message. You were a marionette. Was there something to understand in the humiliation of it? You should try to analyze what was behind Balkoff's and his rebellion, you should try to understand better your Jewish-Canadian inheritance. Igal's voice repeated over and over: You will be part of the ideal of Aguaprieta, Talia. You shall be remembered in Paranaguan history books.

You had a revelation: the happiness, spirit, and personality of Balkoff was dedicated, in his struggle, to others. It was a collective, generalized passion. Everything or nothing, everyone or no one. Transforming the outside world in order to find interior well-being, the symphonic intonation of the human orchestra. Like a revolutionary, to Igal the dream of potential pleasure was more valuable than any real enjoyment from the small and ephemeral glimmer of happiness that (occasionally) a day of life brings. Stabans, on the other hand, lived under the opposite vision: he preferred recognition; in the balance between man and society he inclined toward the individual, never the group (always masturbation, never the orgy). You touched yourself as you thought of them; you caressed your clitoris. Igal knew that things should lead toward global satisfaction, shared by all. For Stabans, life was a succession of ups and downs, the gasping of the deceased, the gradual glide toward the tomb, with misery and little happiness . . . and it could be no other way. Stabans accepted things as they were, he adjusted himself to them and Balkoff, the malcontent, wanted other things.

And you? You respected (and understood) Balkoff, but, without a doubt, you identified with the introspective, pacific, humanist and blessed ideal of Stabans. You preferred a night of passion (and eroticism) to a story of equalitarian justice. You thought then of that Talmudic saying: Better one instant of happiness on earth than a life of bliss in the Great Beyond.

You needed an amulet. G-d was against you, He would make you miserable. Your finger began to move; you were masturbating. The pubis, the clitoris. You closed your eyes, you felt a liquid heat, then you felt someone pulling, from the bottom up, your orgasmic essence.

———

Balkoff was standing in front of you and you took the opportunity to sketch out to him your theory about Jews and the diaspora: "You are a blind Jew, Igal," you said. "In Paranagua they denounce you and they will always denounce you, as a foreigner. They will say you dedicated yourself to mixing into things that don't belong to you, that you rob flour from a sack that is not yours."

"I was born in this city. I am hers and she is mine," he replied.

"It doesn't matter. A Jew is always a citizen from another land—from the Other Land. We are a minority, we are a *rara avis*. We belong nowhere and everywhere, and we don't know who we are."

"Trotsky was a Jew," he said, and talked about his project of redemption. You were calm; your patience had returned. His longings sounded beautiful to you, even though unrealistic, perishable, and condemned to failure.

"Don't talk to me about Trotsky! Look how he ended up, Igal, like a sorry dog. He was an expatriate, like you and me. Your desires are laudable, but acting on them will condemn you to eternal infamy. In fact, you've already taken the steps that have been written, with blood and violent ink, toward your own death sentence."

You waited to see Balkoff's reaction and then you continued: "We are cysts. Jews are so attached to intellectual endeavors because concrete beings inspire in us a profound horror. We have created beautiful ideas, but ideas, remember, are abstractions, absences. What do we idolize? We idolize books, not icons. They will say you kill gentile babies to make *matzoh* for Passover, they will accuse you of villany, of betrayal. Monotheism is an abstraction; it is an invention of man to justify himself and justify his ethical conduct. We are great codifiers of ethics, not promoters of policy. Think about the embarrassment of the Palestine situation . . . look at the incapability we have to put ideas into practice, to concretize them. Think of Disraeli, of Kissinger, or Bar Kokhba. We argued for a promised and controversial land (Palestine), that in reality is the property of all the East, of no one, of the Vatican, of amnesty, of dissension. The idiosyncrasy that fits us best is absence, Igal. Zionism wounds us, nationality wounds us, it wounds us to be citizens, to belong, to form part of something. You love this land (because it's yours, you were born here), but you are, within its vineyards and under the shadow of its mountains, one member more of the Jewish minority, and minorities don't count, they should keep their mouths shut; this game we have to play, this is the price of expatriate existence. Instead of idols, we worship a book, The Book, with capitals "T" and "B." We glorify it. We think it's eternal, that its author is not just anybody, but a Magnanimous Novelist, The Author, the One who knows past, present, and future. We are the characters of a novel that is being written every minute, we're successors of ancestors who began the role, who appeared in the first chapters, and we read those chapters in the synagogue every Saturday. This is our legacy, our responsibility: to continue reading, to continue writing. The Novel that contains us is a pilgrimage, a crossing, like the *Divine Comedy* or *Pilgrim's Progress*. And just like in mystery stories, we don't know the outcome. Your ancestors came to Paranagua by accident. You could just as easily see yourself as a Pole, Argentine, Mexican, Greek, or Canadian. You're a victim of destiny's coincidences, a product of the migratory human waves that work like a lottery, at random. You trust that this is your land but I doubt, frankly, that that's true. You occupy a singular place, privileged, like a citizen of the world, but nobody wants to hear anything more specific. We should continue worshiping our Book. That is our only flag."

"Nice speech, Talia. Too bad you're so mistaken. We cannot continue being pariahs, we have to enter the game, to participate. Looking in from afar is comfortable, but not comforting, and it's not my fault that we live in bubbles far off the ground."

He stayed quiet and then added: "I like you, Talia. We kidnapped you because I wanted to have you near me."

"Liar. It's Stabans who likes me."

"That's possible, but those are just trifles. Me or Stabans, it's all the same to me. Anyway, I'm telling you now that the uprising will be in September. Dalton wants us to make a deal for you, but we don't really even need the ransom. We've raised the sum we need. So I think you should stay at our side, act along with us. You'll become part of history."

Igal left the cell door open behind him when he went out. You saw him go and followed his figure until it had dissipated in the darkness. You thought that you loved him. He represented, for you, praxis, action, courage. When was the last time you had collaborated in a collective project? As a child, you had sneered at youth organizations and camps and had unhesitatingly preferred reading. Life, you know it now, belongs to the believers. Religion signified for you something from the past. Balkoff, on the other hand, was a being of profound faith.

———

You opened the *Sefer ha-Malkuth* and began to read. A chapter spoke of a strange psychiatric case recorded in Chartres, between 1779 and 1780. A poor beggar, probably an immigrant from Algiers to France, had lodged for four nights in a dungeon behind the local cathedral. He was tubercular. He had deep wrinkles on his face, as if someone had drawn them from a map. He had a bowl of soup before he went to sleep. The next morning he was dead; no one claimed his body and he was buried in a common grave the same afternoon. The next night the beggar was once again in the dungeon.

He had risen from the dead. His face was just as furrowed, and he coughed like an animal. The innkeeper was frightened and gave him a pinch to see if he was real. The beggar complained about the lack of service at the inn; the innkeeper once again offered him soup and the next morning, again, he was dead. They buried him once more and once more he returned.

Seven burials in all. The epitaph on his gravestone read as follows: "Jean Jacques Korasa, b. approx. September 1735, d. December 26, 27, & 28, 1779, and January 3, 4, & 9, 1780, Nonbeliever, Immortality is Your Nightmare!" The *Sefer ha-Malkuth* told you, however, that when that last coffin was buried, it was empty. The inhabitants of Chartres had grown weary of celebrating the funeral rites of a man who would not finish dying. You saw that in the last lines of the chapter it was mentioned that in the Koran, in section II, 261, there is a story of an individual whom Muhommed made die over the course of one hundred years. He then brought him back to life. "How long have you been here?" he asked him. "One day, or part of a day."

When one of the two of them, Stabans and Igal, died, would the other half of him disappear as well? The question seemed absurd to you, like a joke. Why were you thinking about such nonsense? It was idleness. You had been there, kidnapped, for weeks, perhaps months. You were like a nervous tiger; you didn't know what to do, whom to bite, what to devour. You raised your head and saw, inscribed in the smooth, white wall in bronze letters, with encrusted diamonds: "Ilan Stavans, b. April 7, 1954, d. August 18, 2033, Evil Jew, Immortality is Your Nightmare!" You rubbed your eyes. Your stomach hurt; it felt like you had a screwdriver or a hammer inside it. How much longer would you be held captive? One day, or a part of a day. You looked again and discovered that there was nothing written on the wall, that you had only imagined it. Then you fell asleep, thinking about the beggar who, in the subway, had looked at you and said in English, *I don't care if it rains or freezes, 'long as I have my plastic Jesus.*

You found a pile of xeroxed papers. They were sitting next to you and you began to read them. They were copies of articles and stories from weekly magazines and local and foreign newspapers, reporting on the robberies of Dalton M. and Igal Balkoff, and they included the pamphlets that had appeared, signed by the Maoists.

Your kidnapping was being discussed at the diplomatic level. The Canadian *Toronto Star* published information about your life there. The prime minister and ambassadors were attempting a dialogue with the presidential cabinet of Paranagua, with no results as of yet. The newspaper *La Jornada* from the city of Narcoprieto included among its pages from September 15 an official communique from the Maoist terrorists: they demanded the removal of the president, the dissolution of the senate, and "clean" elections where intellectual and military members of the left would function as arbiters. The group, calling themselves "Shining Light," would disseminate their ideology through the political party UAP, Utopian Action Party, a group that had little or no influence in Paranaguan political life. Balkoff, Dalton, and some unfamiliar names had signed the manifesto.

They justified their aggressive methods because, they argued, the reality of the country was depressing, licentious, cadaverous, depraved, and bankrupt. They would continue to assassinate police, kidnap foreigners, and demand ransoms until progressive ideals triumphed. You were especially interested in the information about Igal: Name: Igal Balkoff; address: Uxmal 32, Apt. 4, Colonia Narvarte; telephone: 537-3342; date of birth: 9/15/58; place of birth: Paranagua City, Paranagua; education: University of Bellos Aires, 1982, sociology major; graduate courses in political science, Universidad Nacional Autónoma de Paranagua, 1982–1984; working experience: journalist at *La Jornada* and *Excélsior* in 1984; editor of *Ultimas Noti-*

cias supplement "Sabadomingo," contributor to UPI, New York City. The file contained photographs of him when he was a child: cheerful, gentle, with a bow tie and checkered jacket. (Was it Balkoff or Stavans?) Interviews with colleagues and union groups.

Another article (this one you had predicted) spoke of a series of declarations, graffiti, and slogans that had appeared on the walls and in bus terminals of the wealthy sections of Paranagua: Tecamachalco and Rosario, among others. They were anonymous. They denounced Balkoff's Jewishness, they accused him of being a dirty pig, of being idolatrous; they proclaimed him leader of a worldwide Communist conspiracy that planned to take control, without pity or shame, of the world's riches and citizenry. They had been painted with red and blue dripping paint. A few days later, according to another report, a pamphlet had circulated in the Hipódromo, Insurgentes, and Vellavista neighborhoods stating that Igal, with his henchmen, had, three years ago, abducted and killed a Christian infant by the name of Cuauhtémoc Trigo, and had used his blood to make unleavened bread for Passover. The weekly magazines of the right had published caricatures of Balkoff and Dalton, with pointed, aquiline, and exaggerated noses, embracing a uniformed Hitler.

Another xerox copy was of some editorials from *La Jornada;* the opinion was that the Maoist acts were being blown out of proportion. They claimed that the government was using the events to divert attention from more serious and compromising issues. They defended certain Maoists proposals, even some violent ones. You remembered Daniel Stabans's comment, that night at dinner, about the telephone service and how the government fixed the phones to distract people from other things. At the same time, you remembered the flood that had trapped you in the Datsun for five hours. What had happened to your Datsun?

You were afraid; Paranagua was a serpent's nest. There would surely be someone who, with signed letters in the "Correspondence" section, would demand the total expulsion of the Jews, like in Spain in 1492, while others would speak of democracy, tolerance, privilege, acceptance, calm, heterogeneous societies, and peace.

The last text mentioned the curious physical similarity between Igal and Ilan Stabans, a university professor who had disappeared mysteriously two months ago without a trace.

You put the copies aside. Your heart pounded; you begged G-d to forget about you, to leave you in peace. You prayed like you never had before. You wept and felt touched. Time to wise up, you said to yourself.

———

You didn't see Balkoff again. Now it was he who had disappeared. Dalton M. was left in charge of the headquarters at Donceles Street.

The building was old. Its style, colonial, baroque. There were blue and red tiles on the floor. The ceilings were high. The windows were covered with fluttering curtains of gray velvet. The doors squeaked, and none of them (except for the one to your cell) had a handle. On the walls were blisters of humidity up in the corners; the white paint was coming off in rolls, forming cryptic figures, stalactites and scrolls that tangled up where they joined. There were thinning rugs, clean but bunched up, that you tripped over There were lopsided bookcases and shelves. There were glass cabinets and hutches with crystal jars filled with gasoline, crumbs of bread on the ground, dust on the furniture and the curtains. Ancient pieces of wood furniture, wide and swollen. Wide mattresses with soiled sheets. On the table, or when they brought you soup, the silverware was aluminum, the plates pewter. Toilet paper instead of napkins. The water glasses had originally been for candles. The soldiers (and Dalton) prayed to idols and saints to extend and fertilize their luck. There were ugly, faded paintings with aquatic scenes or bucolic, tranquil landscapes with dirty seagulls flying across the sky. All were cheap reproductions, put up hastily for decoration.

The blankets on your bed tasted of the forest (why was that?), as if someone had used them to go camping.

The sounds from the neighboring apartments, the cars, the streetlights that went on religiously every night at 7:00 P.M., the mewl of a cat in some adjacent building, the rag sellers and newspaper boys—you were in your element and you felt part of the atmosphere. The police would be looking for you everywhere, without even suspecting that you were in an obvious place, in the heart of Paranagua. The decision to hide you here, right in the center of the capital, had its advantages: the rooms in this district were, because of their decomposed state, for the most part abandoned. To stay in one of these without going out, for weeks, perhaps months, wouldn't attract any attention. Besides, the area was so well traveled and the hiding place so public, no one would find you there.

You were free to leave your cell, to stroll aimlessly around the hallways, to get to know the place. They had given you some slippers, two changes of clothes, and some jeans that didn't fasten at the waist: bellbottoms like from the seventies. You wandered around, contemplating the objects and the equipment you found there, investigating it all. You had set yourself the task of memorizing the location, the size, the temperature of the things around you, for the simple pleasure of doing it, for the pleasure of challenging your mnemonic capacity. Perhaps you didn't talk to the others, but you let your stream of consciousness out into the open and you talked to yourself, you asked yourself questions, you responded, you disagreed with yourself.

The soup you ate was prepared by a simple soul named Inés López Caballero, a fat, bad-tempered woman with a wandering eye and a finger missing from her left hand. The security and vigilance of the shelter was handled by a cadet (you started to get to know all of them one by one), Renato Ledesma Lima, a young man with curly blond hair who applied butter on the back of his neck to soften it, and who watched the entrance day and night and leaned out the windows to make sure that nobody surprised "Shining Light."

Your calm, and the growing pleasure you got from the air you breathed among your kidnappers, suddenly disappeared when you thought about the insanity of your confinement. You tried to escape two times; both times you failed. Someone you didn't know (a soldier?) caught you red-handed. Dalton beat you the first time; the second time, you got as far as the basement down the back stairs, but when you opened a door you made so much noise breaking a light bulb that they trapped you in an instant. You definitely weren't made for this type of adventure, and you asked yourself how, in Hollywood, people always found a way to escape and did so despite their clumsiness, their level of intelligence, or their disposition. Ever since Balkoff had disappeared, the beatings Dalton gave you had become insistent and brutal, causing bruises on your neck and knees. He was an aggressive stud, violent, macho, and nasty, and you felt degraded and debased; you felt exiled, condemned to a life sentence next to a bull in heat on a mysterious and distant island.

You began, once again, to scream during the night. You suffered from insomnia, you refused to eat, even though you were hungry. You stopped talking and were little by little losing your judgment. Besides, something in your femininity was changing. The sun no longer warmed your bones and the mattress they had put in your cell seemed to you dry, resistant to all comfort.

What was happening with the ransom? Had they contacted your mother and the Reznitskys? Dalton beat you two more times and you answered by kicking him in the balls. They had to tie you to a chair to keep you still. When they untied you, you could have passed for Medusa, Cleopatra or Sheckinah. You masturbated in front of them and cried out for Stabans. You distracted yourself thinking about how the future would invent a camera that could capture, in a flash, an entire life. You read, you picked up pamphlets that were strewn about, or the telephone directory, and memorized them.

In the middle of September they moved you to a different apartment, this one in the Camarek neighborhood, near Chapultepec Park. You still had not seen Igal, not to mention Stavans.

⌒══⌒

You began to get terrible stomach cramps that grew in frequency and intensity in a matter of days; you were also vomiting more.

The apartment in Camarek was smaller than the one on Donceles. They had locked you up in a dark bedroom without any windows and a closet with a store of food from where, you imagined, you were supposed to serve yourself. There also was a bookcase brimming over with books and a desk with folders and notebooks for you to write in, if you had the urge.

You heard that the place on Donceles had become too compromising; the detectives had almost discovered it. Your screams had been heard by two neighbors and the servants of adjoining inhabited buildings. The space in Camarek was larger, with six or more rooms, less humid, more modern (the toilet seat cover was not made of wood like the one on Donceles).

You heard whispering outside the bedroom. Dalton was visited constantly by three civilians (three voices) and various soldiers (you could tell by the stamping of their boots). No news of Balkoff, although you felt he was nearby. You knew that someone was bringing papers and sealed boxes to Dalton; they were piling up in one of the kitchens (there were two) and in the unused bedrooms. Sometimes you would hear the radio of one of the guards or Inés López Caballero, who prepared food as she listened to soap operas. They talked about the fugitive robbers on the news, although less frequently, and about you, Talia, who they guessed to be an ideologist, a voluntary and conscious actor in the holdups. There had been another killing perpetrated by "Shining Light" in Periférico Sur, a commercial center: two civilians dead, cries of horror and a demand, by the hooded men, after taking five hostages and then letting them go, for the resignation of the president.

You heard as well that your mother had come from Montreal to deal directly with your captors. Unbelievable . . . when was the last time she was here? After World War II, in 1946 perhaps. She had returned to Paranagua to save you. Talia, you knew very well that Paranagua is for her the devil's realm; she never liked it. Now she's here because of you, to save your neck. You had told her (although she hadn't listened to you): leave me alone, leave me in peace. When you said it, you still believed that you could be responsible for your own actions. But was that true? Or is it that she would, under the circumstances, have to resolve your life for you?

More whispering and mumbling came in under the door. They came from meetings your kidnappers were holding. Some scheme was afoot, Talia, an event of national scope, something big, immense, bigger than reality, a coup de grace. The coup, you believed, was coming, was near; they were waiting to move at any minute. One could feel the nervousness; footsteps grew quicker; the speakers' voices were rushed. They had obtained enough support and money to put the machine in motion. It was impossible for you to even glimpse the dimensions of the event, Talia, *my* Talia, impossible to define its objectives.

〜━━━〜

It was chilling.

You found another pile of newspapers. By the whiteness of the paper, by the dates, the recentness of the article was irrefutable. The body of Stabans had been found, among many others, in a car crash on the highway to Cuernavaca, sixteen kilometers from Camarek. He was in a bus that had crashed into a train. The driver (according to the police) failed to stop for the light and sped up to pass the train tracks. Seven vehicles had piled up behind the bus in the disaster. A total of seventy-two victims.

Part of Stavans's obituary in *Excélsior:* Ilan Stavans was a professor of Medieval and Renaissance philosophy at the Universidad Autónoma de Paranagua. He had disappeared from his apartment, in Colonia Narvarte, in the middle of July, and a family member had seen him for the last time between Ixtla Ciénfuegos and Donceles streets. A kidnapping had been assumed. Stabans received a master's degree from the Jewish Theological Seminary (New York City), followed by a doctorate in Latin American Letters from Columbia University. Although he lacked a social life, his students and friends knew him to be affable and relaxed. He had published articles about the detective novel and the literary history of Jewish Latin Americans. He had received various grants, among them the Guggenheim Fellowship. His published works included *Franz Rosenzweig's Star of Redemption: An Interpretation* (1983); Babya ibn Paquda's *Manual of Asceticism in the XIIth Century* (1984); *Talia in Heaven: Or, The Book of Dreams* (1989); *The One-Handed Pianist* (1992); *Antihéroes* (1993); and *Tropical Synagogues: Short Stories by Jewish Latin American Writers* (1994). He was also responsible for a metaphysical treaty on holes, a defense of masturbation, and a diatribe on Oscar Wilde. At the time of his death, he was working on a type of joint autobiography. He is survived by his parents, Ofelia and Daniel, and a younger sister, Liora.

The obituary was accompanied by Stavans's photograph, his left hand holding his chin.

You asked yourself: What could he have been thinking when he took his last breath? The limits between the possible and the real had been erased. You doubted everything, the world itself, chronology, and unidimensionality. When had you arrived in Paranagua? And why? Had you ever met Stabans's parents? What did they look like? What did your mother look like, and your brother Amnon? You were no longer yourself. You had more and more stomach cramps. You were nervous, very nervous.

A manuscript had been found in Ilan's luggage. Title: *Sefer ha-Malkuth: Or, The Book of Dreams*. A fireman had saved it at the scene of the accident and a reporter copied the following page in order to publish it as a testament: "What are the things that seem to me most strange? Not the most trivial. These produce in me an affect as if they were trying to speak to me. They exasperate me, like someone struggling to read the twisted lips of a paralyzed man, without succeeding. For me the world is filled with silent voices. Which secret words do we hide away? In which language do we speak to each other? Do inanimate objects experience hallucinations? Truth does not always manifest itself in images; it is feasible that it presents itself to us through stories and through lies. Lies are the things that are to me least trivial. Human character is the thing that is to me the strangest."

A journalist from *La Jornada* had elaborated on the theme of lies, inquiring into whether Stabans were related to Igal Balkoff, saying that he looked like his twin, his cousin or brother. He had compared two photographs, of Stabans and of Balkoff in the bank, wounded, and had commented on them.

At that time, you heard on the radio that another batch of anti-Semitic allegations were appearing on walls and in doorways. "Death to the Jews," said one, with a swastika next to it. "Jews," said another, "Christ's murderers."

The disturbance made you explode: you smashed a mirror, you crumpled up the newspaper, you chewed it up and swallowed it. The death of a loved one is the most intolerable horror that a body can hold. The only thing worse would be one's own death.

Why did G-d create human beings? you asked yourself. To kill them. Stabans had died, was dead. Was it possible? How had the *Sefer ha-Malkuth* gotten into his hands? You thought that maybe two copies existed, you thought that nature commits errors, that ubiquity exists. You searched in your belongings that you had in the apartment on Donceles Street. It wasn't there. You asked the cadets, you asked Inés, Dalton M. Nothing: no book, no Stabans, and no Balkoff.

You slept, and when you awoke you searched, among the surviving newspapers (the ones you hadn't devoured in your delirium), for one that would tell you the whereabouts of your book.

✦━━━━✦

You found it a few days later. What did you read there? The chapter that spoke about "the peculiar crudeness that is a hole." What is a hole? asked the *Sefer ha-Malkuth*. The diameter of a cannon, the emptiness of a circle or any dug-out cavity, a nose, a parenthesis, a vagina, any bottle or ring. It is the space between two points, the air between the filaments, a scar, the absence of matter, a hat, a doughnut, a diving helmet, the cry of an infant, a set of dentures, a noose, a throat. What's a hole? In the course of his existence, man has in front of him an emptiness that follows him and longs to embrace him. That emptiness is a hole, an abyss, oblivion, madness, or perversity. From birth to death, we defy, with words and with acts, this dimension, this hole: we spit on it, we taunt it. But the hole does not disappear because it is infinite intelligence, it is time and truth. It is, and against it there is nothing. In fact, it will be this hole that, in the end, will sink its claws into us and we will disappear.

You were so sure, Talia, so completely sure, that heaven was also a hole.

✦━━━━✦

You held the *Sefer ha-Malkuth* close to you; you kissed it. You leafed through it, as if looking for the ultimate secret. You saw that it presented two riddles throughout: it avoided writing out the word G-d, and it wrote in numbers, never in letters, the numbers (except for the number one, synonym of unity).

Why?

Response number one: if man is an attribute of the thing, he has it in his power. To know or to manipulate numbers is to dominate objects or individuals. To know who the author of the *Sefer ha-Malkuth* is was the same as knowing why one has been written in its pages. Response number two: you thought that in the sum of its numbers, you would find the keys and the mysterious name of its author (who, according to the obituary published in *Excélsior*, was Stabans, but you knew that to be false).

You forgot about that theory of the Spirit as the anonymous author of everything and you began to count, spelling out the numbers. You began, as well, in a vengeful manner, to complete the word G-d every time it appeared.

In Camarek (a neighborhood located a few kilometers from the Citadel and the Aguaprieta National Palace), you would finally see Balkoff. The fright that seized you is indescribable. He was smoking in a relaxed way. He was dressed in a psychedelic vest, his boots were caked with mud, his pants were ragged and torn, his hair uncombed, and the beard an imitation of the Amazon River in its size and bushiness.

Why hadn't he died in the car crash?

One morning there was Balkoff, drinking a cup of coffee. He came over to you and you spit on him; you took his cup and poured the coffee on his clothes. You looked at each other and you howled: Is this meant to mortify my curiosity or to conquer it? Am I supposed to know who I am—if ever it was meant for me to be somebody? Bloody Edward Hyde.

You tried to unbutton his pants and raise up his shirt. You wanted to prove that Igal still had (or not) the scar on his stomach, caused by the gun shot in the bank. You kicked him to the ground and bit him, and Balkoff saw that your belly was swollen. He squeezed you tightly and then calmed your spirit, while he slapped you on the cheeks to rouse you out of your frenetic trance.

Bloody Hyde! Bloody Hyde! you were saying. Hyde? Balkoff was disoriented.

"You're wrong, Talia," he yelled at you, "they have to get you back to the Reznitskys as soon as possible. The ransom must come through quickly. If not this delirium of yours will fall on us, along with the burden of your unexpected pregnancy."

The ransom was paid.

Your body appeared battered, with scratches on your legs and chest. A shopkeeper found it in an empty parking lot in the colonia of Nixtamal. It was wrapped in a plastic bag, tied with rope, and had been propped up against a trash can. It smelled. The shopkeeper at first suspected you were dead but he put a mirror up to your nose and when it steamed, he saw that you were merely unconscious. He called the police and they arrived, accompanied by journalists and photographers. You skirt was stained with motor oil and blood. Your feet were burned and blistered. Your shoes, put on by force, had string and straw stuck to them. You were pallid and bruised. Your hair, stiff and matted. When and how had they tortured you? You didn't remember.

Your mother arrived at the scene of the crime, cried, and took you to the Bagé Hospital, where your brother Amnon, Daniel and Ofelia Stavans, and the Reznitskys, all anxious about you, went to see you. You heard them from a distance, as if enclosed in a space capsule.

The doctors operated on you to extract a minuscule piece of some mineral substance, in the shape of a symmetrical polyhedron, that was embedded in one knee and that seemed to be digging a hole in you. During the operation, you dreamed that they were inserting a glass filled with liquor in your belly. You saw crystals around you, multicolored crystals moving in and out of place like in a kaleidoscope.

You were put in room number 666 in the hospital; it was filled for the week of your convalescence with friends and acquaintances, lawyers and journalists. You came back to yourself on the third day. By then your pregnancy was known by all. While people nearby talked to you, you were thinking that once again you had lost the *Sefer ha-Malkuth*. Your heart palpitated. Should you look for it again? Yes, and you did so with terror. Providence, now you understood, had obliged your precious book to be and not to be your pet, to be with you and not with you. You rummaged around everywhere with your eyes. No, you had left it in Camarek.

Your mother contacted a lawyer, Jeremías Seamslow, and he began to move the necessary papers so that your departure from Paranagua could happen as soon as possible. The national government, considering you an aggressor, spy, persona non grata, a traitor tourist, impeded the process. Federal police sent by the president came into your room and appealed to you, but you neither spoke nor made a sign. You were mute. Your lips were like a tomb; in fact, you opened your mouth just one time, one night, when you mumbled the contents of a terrifying nightmare: you were in an onion and saw the world from all angles and from none. You had daydreams, wet hallucinations. One morning you woke up in a sweat, sure that you were a parenthesis.

The possibility of losing your baby was real because your resistance severely affected during the kidnapping, could not satisfy both your needs: you ate badly and digested worse. You found out, then, that Paranaguan law prohibits abortion.

Later you contracted an infection in your knee and another operation was required. When finally you had your strength back, you laughed. What else could you do? You put on some lipstick that was on your dresser and daubed your eyelashes and mouth, and with a blue marker you drew concentric circles on your cheeks. When you saw your mother (who spent the greater part of the day at your side), you felt separated from your own body and an omnipotent voice spoke to you from your insides: travelling to such unstable places as Paranagua is dangerous, Talia. You should not have come. It is preferable to live comfortably, to resist change. One can grow stupid, don't you think? One can go mad.

⌐———,

Jesus Christ. Why had you thought about Jesus Christ during the bone-breaking scene in the Narvarte apartment? Jesus Christ on the cross taught us to love suffering and it was he who began to corrupt that cursed word: *love*.

Love: Petrarch, Plato, Leone Ebreo, Goethe. Love, synonym of sacrifice, of devotion, of renouncement, rape, subtlety, forgetfulness, oblation, holocaust, libation, renouncement, abandon, offerings, immolation, affection, tenderness, adoration, religiosity, evangelization, death. Animals want sex, not love. We humans are the only ones to infuse something frightening into love: responsibility.

Love and responsibility. We turn sexuality into a sanctuary; we limit it and legitimize it. Chance, mating, palpitation, pleasure. Energy is controlled, trained. Jesus Christ is the receptacle for human love—deprivation of something that belonged to others that he tried to symbolize in its totality. You had loved—for what?

You thought: *Talia. Talia Among Men. Talia in Heaven.* What beautiful names for a novel. Someone, some unknown person, one with talent, should look for a quiet place and sit down to describe your adventure. Without a doubt there would be enough material to work with. Too bad you hadn't kept a careful and precise diary of the details, of your spiritual ups and downs, of the passions, the joys and miseries. You had the necessary material but you squandered it, you fool. The world is here to be counted, to be turned into narration, Talia.

Sadness. Was love the message of the novel in which you were perhaps living? *Talia: A Love Story.* Love is velvety, corny, pagan. You had loved with passion, devoted to physical worship, to momentary advantage, without responsibility, given to hedonism, and now you had not even a bastion of reserve. Love; but love for whom? Of what? You belonged to no one, not even to yourself. Who were you? What did you look like? You had idolized your father, you had loved Stavans. Silence, resignation; both had ended as absences, buried, lifeless. On the other hand, you had had Balkoff, who, although a Jew, focused his love on a modern Jesus Christ: the redemption of the masses. Now you understood him better than ever; you identified with him. He was a man who had a reason to live, something to long for. Balkoff, *your* Balkoff.

Jesus Christ—sensibility. You were replete with sensibility; you let yourself feel moved for the things in your reach; these experiences generated knowledge, but from there forward you would find obstacles. Knowledge to what end? With what objective? Judeo-Christian society is a ladder of sensibility: Jesus Christ taught us about suffering, and later Spanish chivalrous literature and romantic poetry disposed us to the discovery of love; from that love that is a strange sentiment, difficult to describe, uncomfortable, an invention of the West. Yes, we infuse something horrible into love: responsibility, responsibility between lovers, responsibility to a family. The lover feels his beloved depends on him; the bourgeois family makes us feel nostalgic for home, the nostalgia of the maternal kiss and of well-being, overprotection, comfort; it teaches us that guilt is everywhere. Love and guilt, two sides of the same coin.

Would you have a child, Talia? You were pregnant, pregnant, you were, you were pregnant. G-d would incubate in your womb a monster, a fearsome ogre, a creature of the darkness. Another title for your novel: *Talia Against Heaven*. A worm would come forth from your belly; yes, a worm; it would be *your* child and the child of your sensibility, of your love for your mother and the guilt you felt toward and because of her. A Jew who longs for and is made anxious by the suffering of Christ; that's what you are, Talia, a Christianized Jew.

Why did you think of Jesus Christ that day in the apartment? Perhaps it was a premonition: you began to gestate, to incubate your novel.

Whose child were you carrying? Was it logical to think that it was Ilan Stabans's? You preferred the possibility of Balkoff and visualized him as the father. You visualized him, as well, with his project of utopia. And if he fulfilled his promises?

Igal was an authentic revolutionary. Revolutions, you had heard so much about them. In Canada, social change came through elections and reforms. In Paranagua, only after violent attacks. There was no other way to change the national chaos into something else. You thought that revolutionaries and their revolutions belonged to the realm of fantasy: they break the routine, they dare to make order from disorder, to move in the sphere of the impossible. They have the vague hope of "bettering" reality and invariably end in failure because they come replete with impetuousness, hastiness, and they end, either becoming greedy and abusing power, or simply die.

You said to yourself: you have to learn to see things in another way. It is impetus, and not its consequences, that matter. A revolution is an accident, it is painful to experience but once the wound scars over, things go back to the way they were. The scar is the evidence of the eruption but only the eruption; in the instant that it comes to be, a validity is reached. The world goes on and will go on the same. Dreamers are necessary, nevertheless, and hopes must continue. Only because it's hopeless is hope given to us.

It was the end of the week of your convalescence that you found out, in the middle of October, from a headline in *Excélsior*, what it was that had so alarmed the city and turned the government upside down: "Uprising in Aguaprieta; 132 Dead; 87 Taken Hostage; National Palace in Rebel Hands." You read that Igal Balkoff and Dalton M. were the protagonists of that uprising and commanded a retinue of dozens of mercenaries. The objective was to take the citadel and seize the Aguaprieta Palace. They had almost reached their goal.

The usual guards had been watching the buildings in the area and around Chapultepec Park. Nobody had been prepared for the incident. Some soldiers were asleep, others playing cards. They were taken by surprise and there were gunshots. By coincidence, a patrol car on the prowl had shown up and defended the rearguard. The rebels, with no other choice, had to console themselves with the Aguaprieta National Palace and sacrifice the preferred target: the office of the secretary of state, in the northeast section of the citadel. When they arrived at the palace, they rushed the doors, climbed the stairs, shooting on sight, and set a red and white flag fluttering up on the roof. Voices cried out for peace and liberty, asked forgiveness for so much violence, and then kept on killing. They looked (at least in the press photos) happy and satisfied.

Reports surfaced about the palace: it was located to the east of the city of Paranagua. In the past it had been a fort that served as headquarters for independence fighters in 1912, against the Spanish armada, and in 1961 it had been turned into a museum. There was discussion as to why "Shining Light" had chosen this place: it was three kilometers away from the government administrative center, from where the country was governed. The distance from one to the other was a quick jump.

You read too that the attack was carried out in nine cars (the Volkswagen they had kidnapped you with in Tecamachalco among them) and two armored tanks, robbed from some army squadrons by a few deserting soldiers. The stampede lasted seventeen minutes in total.

The aggressors' organization, it was asserted, was remarkable; they had planned everything, everything but the presence of the patrol car. In the trunks of their cars they had kept bombs, which were used immediately. The attackers fired aimlessly, the police counterattacked, and four attackers died while the police, the soldiers, and even civilians fell like flies, in substantial numbers.

A shipment of munitions, dynamite, pistols, machine guns, and grenades had been unloaded (said *La Jornada*) by Igal Balkoff two kilometers away. In Camarek, where you had been staying, one day earlier, three attackers piled boxes with supplies on the first floor of the Aguaprieta Palace, while the others were winning the battle. The building was occupied so quickly, even in spite of the exertion, that the aggressors still had enough energy to proclaim themselves the new government of the country. Their sermon confirmed (visibly) the liberation of Paranagua from the oppressor's yoke.

Upon learning of the incident, you kept the television on at all times. You heard sometime later that a bullet had reached Dalton (the front-page photograph published the second day was of him) and the group, who had taken as hostages various employees of the museum, had let two or three go, due to heart conditions. They had the rest under constant watch.

Once again you felt like an accomplice: the boys, your kidnappers, who had tortured you and driven you mad, had done it, had fulfilled their promise. Your preaching and sermons to Balkoff had been in vain, had lacked sense. You remembered his long hair tied back with bandannas, his bushy beard, the figures that the smoke of his cigarette made when he visited your cell. You remembered that day when you poured the coffee on him. Wasn't he perhaps braver than Stabans, who had died stupidly in a car crash? You felt admiration, surprise, and you applauded Balkoff.

The incredible reign had taken hold of Paranagua. A revolution, or at least a coup of honor, had germinated in your presence. You had been witness, you had followed to the last detail every intrigue, every desire, every injustice. Pride, there was pride in your soul, pride and complicity. Incredible. You doubted that the rebels would get much further: revolutions go, revolutions come; how and when will we save ourselves? Never, although it's worth the try.

You stayed quiet; not one word crossed your lips.

You wanted to call the Stabanses. They had visited you a few times during the first days of your convalescence. They looked thin, dazed. They talked about Ilan with your mother, of his work as a university professor, the affection his students had for him, the way they felt possessed by his words. Your mother watched them suspiciously, perhaps thinking that that diabolic Ilan had deflowered your existence, your goodness. The Department of Religious Sciences at the Universidad Autónoma de Paranagua had organized an homage to him, where colleagues, journalists, writers, and friends had participated with lamentations and tears. His unexpected death had been a tragedy. A healthy man with much potential. The accident that nature had caused broke his creative sequence, and stopped frozen, once and for all, a promising career as a critic, thinker, and teacher. They were crying, they looked to be in pain. You listened, without participating; you laughed and you doubted. Were Ilan and Igal one person or weren't they? Apparently, for the Stabanses, the answer was no, they were two distinct people. Ofelia looked at you out of the corner of her eye, as if wishing that, now, you would show some honor and devotion to the memory of her son. She approached you and asked forgiveness for the way she had treated you that last time, when you argued about the two personalities of her son, and did not dare to speak about your romance with her first born. She didn't because she felt that you had discovered the weak side, the defect that pushed you away from him, that it would break the bond between the two of you. Perhaps, as well, she didn't because she was envious—you, Talia, were in the present the feminine image that she had so loved to be in the past with her son. They were contradictory feelings that let themselves come to the surface of her heart that day in her house, drinking coffee (which had tasted cold to you, although it steamed). You listened to it all, Talia, everything, without emitting a sound.

You asked yourself: if Ofelia thought before that her son had two faces, how had she managed to convince herself of the contrary? Daniel talked to you about that dinner, of the traffic jam in your Datsun caused by the torrential storm that had rained down from the sky. You felt in your insides a deep affection for the Stabanses; you loved them and, at the same time, you blamed them for not having told you the truth when it was necessary. Then you immediately remembered (once again) being at Budget Rent-a-Car in Montreal your conversations in the Portuguese restaurant, the bottles of wine and the delicate cakes; you remembered the mirror that morning before meeting them, when you found your first wrinkles, when you realized that you would never again be a girl.

What about Liora? you wanted to ask, and you got your answer when she herself came to see you four days later. She seemed intimidated by something, skittish. But even so, how beautiful she was! you thought. How attractive! Her small good face spoke to you of naivete, innocence, immaturity, the fire that burns when we are young and know nothing of the details of the labyrinth that is the universe. You sincerely wanted to talk to Liora, to look for yourself in her gestures, in her concealments, but you stopped yourself, you waited; now is not the moment.

Soon after, through some incomprehensible doings, the Stabanses and Liora stopped visiting or calling on the phone, and as you learned more about the news of the attempt at Aguaprieta, you knew you had to break the silence and go see them. But you let the seconds pass by, the hours, the days.

When you were feeling better, your lawyer, Seamslow, managed to get the papers completed to get you out of Paranagua. At the end of October you would fly to New York and be admitted for a general physical at Mount Sinai Hospital. Your mother was tired of Paranagua; she had nothing but curses for the country and its people; she complained about the food, the taxi service, the overpopulation and the impossible condition of public phones.

And you, did you want to leave? You didn't know. Maybe yes and maybe no. So the rocky chapters of your novel about the search for yourself would be left behind: *Talia Absorbed*. Had this trip been a vision of hell? An amorphous, convex, simulated hell, replete with riddles and doubts. What is certain is that you wanted to return to a normal rhythm, that you needed a cleansing. Your mother and Amnon obsessively tried to convince you to erase these months in Paranagua from your memory. A lie, because no one can erase from their side a constantly pestering buzz. It is and it will be there, forever. Taking a risk, you thought the opposite: it was the key to a life that would never be the same. Besides, the baby-worm that had nailed itself inside you was the link between your time in Paranagua and your future.

◦━━━◦

New York did not come so soon.

Paranagua was in a state of emergency. It was ridiculous, but "Shining Light," with their eighty-two hostages, had the national government with their back against the wall. They asked (again), with determination and without disillusion, always optimistically, for the resignation of the entire presidential cabinet and the immediate naming of an interim administration that would come from a (not very extensive) prepared list of artists and intellectuals that was made public in *La Jornada*. Old photographs of Dalton and Balkoff appeared continuously on the televi-sion screen. The event was the talk of the town; it was discussed in cafes, at roundtables, in editorials, television news commentaries, and even the international press bombarded Aguaprieta and Chapultepec Park, looking for news to spread, analyzing the economic and political reality of Paranagua, putting in context the sudden event that had thrown off the fragile collective equilibrium.

Of course the demands of "Shining Light" were ignored. You could have predicted it. What pained you most, however, was the third wave of anti-Semitic proclamations that emerged, daily, during the third week of

October, in the form of graffiti and posters. They were intentionally trying to create the epitaphs of a Jewry that, according to the anonymous denouncers, "should pay for the revolutionary nightmares of one of their most asinine members." They spoke of the historical evil of Israel, of the Jews' spiritual perversity, of their rejection of Christianity, of being idolatrous, materialistic, and simpletons. Within a few weeks a synagogue in Rosario was desecrated, its four *Torahs* burned. Also, seven tombstones in the Jewish cemetery of Tecamachalco were found, one rainy morning at the beginning of November, destroyed, their stones painted black and covered with swastikas. There was an atmosphere of repression, violence, dispiritedness, suffocation, and misery in Paranagua.

It was difficult for you to know if national public opinion was with or against the rebels. Probably half and half. You felt that the uprising would attract, among the people you knew, as much sympathy as detractors. People were always fascinated by deeds; they followed the news without blinking. They asked what would happen if the government gave in, what would happen if the exchange of hostages was made under such conditions that they allowed for Balkoff's and Dalton's freedom, and permitted them to escape from the country. There was uncertainty, anxiety to know how and when the incident would end. The government, meanwhile, acting like nothing was going on, tried to maintain calm.

You had your baggage ready to go. Your mother had packed it with your help. You had left the hospital and were staying at the Hilton Hotel, on Reformación Street. The bill would be paid up in the next few days. Amnon was buying handicrafts at the markets to take back as presents, so you were waiting for him. In every other way, you were ready. You had begun to recover your voice; you were reincorporating yourself into the world's order. You had resigned yourself, you had to leave, to see other lights, to heal yourself, to get better. You had to start again, to be born a different Talia. What could stop you?

A telegram over the phone. They called you to tell you the worst possible news: Liora had been murdered.

It was (another) retaliation. An eye for an eye and a tooth for a tooth. Ofelia described the incident to you in an unyielding lament: Liora had left an Afro-Antilles dance class at 7:00 p.m., in a commercial area of Narvarte, when some drunken soldiers had suddenly grabbed her, pushed her into an empty building, beat her, and fatally stabbed her. Why Liora? you asked. When she had visited you in Bagé, you said, you had seen fear in her. Yes, said Ofelia, ever since that article in *La Jornada* about the connection between her dead brother Ilan and Igal Balkoff, her friends from the León Shestow School, some of them very poor, began to verbally attack her. They had intimidated her, they had screamed "Jewish whore," and Liora had stopped going to class; she was nervous and had diarrhea for a week. They had followed her, caught her by surprise, and had fulfilled their promise of revenge. The killers had left written on her clothes: "*Domenio Evreo* of Paranagua." While the words were obscured, not so its message.

You went to the burial, along with Amnon and your mother. It was held in the same cemetery where Ilan was buried, the one which had been desecrated. The congregation, approximately one hundred among families, friends, and strangers, were whispering to each other, and you heard that some of them planned to leave the country that same day, to go to Texas, Miami, France, or Israel. The current situation was too dangerous, the assassinations could repeat themselves. Paranagua was turning into a giant trap. You also realized that many didn't know that Liora's death had something to do with an anti-Semitic act. Ofelia, so as not to cause more trouble, had started the rumor that some delinquents, trying to steal her wallet, had killed her. The grieving took over—grieving and desperation. There were many handkerchiefs and lilies.

After it was over, you went to see Stabans's grave. The hillocks of sand were still fresh and a wooden plaque announced his name and dates of birth and death. You had predicted August sixth; he had died on the eighth (the sixth, someone told you, was Ofelia's birthday). Whose body had they buried there? You thought that, in his duplicity, Igal/Ilan had played a joke on everyone. You smiled, and before leaving, you placed a small stone on the wood.

You walked toward the exit. You waited for the embraces to finish and you walked over to Ofelia.

⁕━━━⁕

"I'm so sorry for what happened!"

"The tragedy—two children in a few months—we were a happy family, you're a witness to that. Daniel and I are heartbroken, Talia. What went wrong? Where did we make a mistake?"

"We Jews are always guests," you said and then were quiet for a minute. Then: "I want to see Balkoff, to see if I can get some answers."

"Why an accident? What was Ilan doing on a bus coming from Cuernavaca?"

"I have a slight feeling that Ilan is alive."

"Please, Talia, let it go. I can't take any more."

"I want to speak with Igal Balkoff at the Aguaprieta Palace. I don't know who to contact, how to do it. I need the army to protect me. I think I can persuade Balkoff and Dalton M. that their revolution will fail and will end in defeat. It's my duty as a Jew to try. You might even get your family back, Ofelia." You waited. "You should have told me about Ilan's double identity."

You knew that the Paranaguan army was ready to attack Aguaprieta, whatever the cost, saving or sacrificing the hostages. The occupation of "Shining Light" was too much, it had to be settled at once.

"Fine, I don't want to make things worse," you said. "Can you help me to get in contact with the general who is behind the liberation operation and the return of the palace, Ofelia? It's essential."

"I don't know anybody."

You didn't know what to do. You said goodbye. When you got into a taxi with your mother and brother, you asked the driver to take you to Camarek; you had to take care of something important before you left. You were suspicious about something; you threw a tantrum and finally they a-greed to go. You drove around the colonia, looking for a building that looked like the one you had stayed in, for something you recognized. You drove around for ages and found nothing. The images of the burial left a dull taste in your mouth, depressing in your memory. All three of you were in a bad mood.

Finally, you convinced your mother to have the driver take you to Agua-prieta. They left you a few blocks away from the palace. You got out of the car and began to walk. You spoke with some officials, with a detective. They recognized you from the newspaper photographs. You said that you were going to try to talk to Igal Balkoff and would try to persuade him to aban-don his position and give up. That way they would save many lives and the army would come off looking like heroes.

One of them communicated with a central office and passed on your message. Meanwhile, as you arranged your meeting, a nostalgia overcame you because, up to this point, nothing had pleased you more than the tri-umph of the Aguaprieta uprising. You saw it as a coronation, the last sal-vation through a Faustian coordination of irreverence and errors. But victory was improbable and you had to stop the final killing scene as best you could; your affection for the Stabanses and for Igal Balkoff obliged you. You had to stop, in any way you could, the anti-Semitism floating through Paranagua.

Very well, they would let you try. They dressed you in a bulletproof vest, gave you a watch-microphone, and took you to the palace, accompa-nied by two motorcycles as escorts. You were in a luxurious limousine, the type reserved for diplomats. When you were nearing the door, you saw a line of soldiers, tanks, and cannons, all the artillery ready to fire. You got out of the car and walked a few steps toward the fortified palace.

You had read something about the architecture of the palace. It was built in Gothic style. It would have fit perfectly near Amiens Cathedral, in France, or in Venice, next to Dux Castle. It was of enormous dimensions. Arches and horse stables surrounded it, and farther on the woods of Chapultepec Park. You saw high pillars juxtaposed on the roof. It was, without a doubt, a fascinating construction. The reinforcements and flying buttresses formed an armor of stone. There were also great and numerous windows. It was built like a labyrinth; you could have lost yourself inside.

You still remember its majestic form. To dim the excess light, there were stained glass windows with religious figures. They were surrounded by capitals, gargoyles, archivolts, spires, ashlars of wood, bronze weathervanes, tapestries, church ornamentation, and old smithery and ceramics works. As the door slowly opened (you could see, as you rang the bell two times), there was, in a garden, a fabulous sculpture of a smiling angel, holding a bow and arrow, with its legs crossed and admiring one of its feet. In front of you was an esplanade, and farther on a tunnel that connected the building with the citadel.

A wall with battlements and stone merlons (some of them chipped, or with posters announcing theatrical events or union strikes) prevented onlookers from seeing in. A beautiful drawbridge had functioned in the eighteenth century, but now was permanently in a horizontal position. There were chapels, turrets, watchtowers, observation windows, and cold wall, made of wide and heavy blocks. You raised your eyes. A soldier was aiming a gun a you from a nearby tower. You thought he was going to shoot. You shouted your name from afar and raised up to the four winds a red and white flag.

Nothing happened.

You rang the bell again. You waited five minutes. The door remained closed. You could hear a shot from inside and the barking of a dog. Everyone was waiting, the soldiers and the rebels (who had somehow been warned of your arrival). You turned around to look behind you.

The squadron chief was ready, if anything happened to you, to charge immediately, quickly, without delay. Your agreement with them, with the government, was that your life was in your own hands, that you were running your own risk with whatever you decided to do. They agreed to employ you as an emissary, believing you could settle accounts and resolve the setback. But if you died, it would matter little or nothing to them.

It had rained the night before and was threatening to do so again. Another shot into the air. You didn't know what to do. Your pregnancy could bring about unexpected consequences. Your stomach hurt.

The second door, near a parapet, opened and the first thing you saw was a brown cat. You paused, and then you went in.

You saw peasants and soldiers everywhere waiting for orders. They were bored, hungry, and dissatisfied.

One man with a straw hat, a Zapata-style moustache, and a cartridge belt gave you instructions. He signaled with the end of his finger where you should go. He spoke a broken Spanish, very coarse. You went up some stairs and turned toward the right. There were soldiers with machine guns all around. They looked tired, overwhelmed. Their eyes followed you. There were doors that opened and closed, with people carrying munitions and the wounded. You heard noises; where were the hostages?

A large room was waiting for you at the end of a hallway, under a stained glass window of the Virgin of Guadalupe next to a lamb. You heard, from inside the room, a grave voice calling you.

⸺

"I'm exhausted, Igal. I'm not here to argue. I'm not asking for an explanation because I admire what you've done. I've learned to respect the anguish of a man who lives in conflict with his circumstances, not with himself. I'm here for other reasons," you told him shyly, urgently, imperatively, almost denouncing.

The atmosphere was somber. A dog barked endlessly outside and you imagined it to be enormous. In front of you you could make out the figure of a massive yet weak individual, voluminous though aged, sitting at a desk with revolvers, a pair of ballpoint pens, a hand grenade, and a handkerchief.

He had a diffident mien; he held his head down and smoked eagerly. His spinal column was stiff and stooped. The denseness of his beard made it clear he had renounced shaving or shaping it in any way. Or worse, that he was half man, half wolf. Hair grew like down on his chest, under his arms (he was wearing a sleeveless undershirt) and on his forearms. You would have sworn it was not Balkoff. There was something different in this man, something. What was it? His smell perhaps, of wet cement or mutton fat, or maybe the pallid color of his skin, gray, like slightly bruised lilac.

Who was it then? Gray, gray was his character as well. There was no light in the room and it was the hour that brings night with it. The backlighting of a window erased his gestures, turned them into shadow. He was a silhouette, the smoke of a ghost. The man hummed a melody. What music was that? You didn't recognize it. It was impossible to tell if it was Stabans or the other one, or both. You perceived with more strength a range of odors that you could barely categorize: rotted wood, sulphur, starched sheets, incense, chopped onion, and wet dust (love dust?). The man's face was disfigured. No, neither Stabans nor Balkoff, but someone else, someone in between, neither rogue nor martyr, neither dreamer nor gentleman.

His hair had grayed. He was an old man. He had on his upper arm a tied bandage with some blood splashed over it.

"Talia, what's goin' on?"

The same question. That interior voice that had been speaking recently told you that this meeting, accidental although predetermined, was included in the record of heaven, that it would have come to pass even in spite of the Paranaguan government, even in spite of any other adversity. Both lived for each other, they were there to justify their existences. You remembered how you had asked permission of the generals and detectives to enter Aguaprieta. The permission had been granted more easily than you had expected. Why? Because the meeting had been planned by nature, like in the story of the rabbi's son and the devil. You stayed silent. On the other side of the door to the room there was an oblong, yellowed mirror. You saw it and tried to look at yourself to prove that you were really there, that you weren't a specter.

You saw in the reflection both images, yours and his. You also saw that there was an old and heavy book on the desk, next to the revolvers; it was your copy of the *Sefer ha-Malkuth*.

You said: "Your fucking revolution turned me into a celebrity, killed your sister, and made Paranagua anti-Semitic. Can you believe that? Look at me! I can save you from a dreadful catastrophe but you have to do what I say."

"Dalton is dead. He was shot in the liver. We tried to help him. One of the soldiers is a doctor and knows first aid. We couldn't; he left us. I'm alone, Talia." He rose up and walked around the office. He limped; he reminded you of Quasimodo. Grains of sugar or sand scattered on the floor crushed under his shoes and made you raise your head, as if hypnotized. The sound made you wince, it curled your skin.

"Listen to me," you went on. "Who put you inside me, in my veins? How many faces do you hide?" An intruder knocked on the door. It was a messenger bringing a note. Balkoff (or Stavans, or Balkoff "and" Stabans) read it and the messenger looked at you briefly and then left.

"Talia Kahn, you're a hysterical Jew," your ex-lover said.

"They're going to kill you, Stabans."

"It's all a dream. The catastrophe began long ago."

He was silent. You were anxious. You thought quickly about the thunder of the cannons that waited outside. You asked him: "Who are you?"

"I am the world that will gradually hurl down to an emptiness and that, in its evolution, obliges us to trust in individuality. Monotheism, monogamy, monographs, galactic unity, et cetera."

"I don't understand."

"Don't schizophrenics perhaps enjoy the privilege of being one and many at the same time? I am many men and no one. I am a polygamist, because I loved you many times. I am idolatrous, because I believe more than one time in *God*. I am in exile, because I live simultaneously outside and inside my body."

The words stopped and the silence returned. Outside the rain had begun. You saw the drops that slid down a stained glass window depicting a pastoral scene of St. Peter. In the future, you would remember Paranagua as the city of rain. It was beautiful that heaven was dripping down once again, like a present, like it did on the day you met Ilan Stabans in his parents house, or like the afternoon he made love to you with such delight and later turned into the brute that had come to dominate him. *Talia and the Rain.*

A dog barked and was joined by two others, more piercing.

"We can leave together. They'll kill you, just like they killed Talia. . . ." It was a slip. " . . . just like they killed Liora." What had made you say your own name?

"Leave for where? My death began months ago."

Then you told him the truth. You told him you were pregnant. Silence.

"Only because it is hopeless is hope given to us," he replied.

You repeated the phrase and responded: "Leave with me. We can escape through the back way. I have a baby inside me, I want you to see it born, to be with it. We Jews will never know how to adjust ourselves to an expatriate existence. We will never fit in the established order of things. Our complaints are never as legitimate as the rest. We can long for things, but not concretely, because that is not allowed us. Paranagua has killed Liora. What killed her was the icy knife of a young man from León Shestowo high school (where you recruited your mercenaries), but the responsibility belongs to all, we breathe it together. Your place is not in this revolution, nor in any other. If you have to live in Paranagua, your life must be lived anonymously, as a guest, a colleague, never as a citizen with equal rights and obligations."

You thought the conversation would last longer. You had so much to say. Your love had twisted you, you were furious, you had been a victim of your captors and of Stabans; that time in the cell, he had promised you that none of this would cause you any pain. That had been a lie. You wanted to hit him and to kiss him.

In fact, you had learned to love him as he was, ephemeral, ethereal, transient, heterogeneous, polymorphous, abstract, volatile, polytheistic, polygamous, and polysemic. "I have to leave Paranagua," you said. "My mother can't stand it any longer, she wants to see me free of all this."

"It doesn't matter. In any case, you were just passing through," he said sardonically.

"Don't make fun of me!"

"Sometimes we bring others, without wanting to, into the intentions of our acts."

"It was written that you and I would cross paths."

"Perhaps."

"How can you give Liora her life back?"

Another silence. He/they began to sob and you saw a tear running down his/their cheek/s.

"Give it up, Balkoff," you heard someone whisper. The man began to shake. He had sat down and got up once again, smashing more grains of sugar or sand beneath his feet. You heard again the sound of bones breaking and again witnessed the transformation with rapt attention.

His hair grew long, his skin folded up, its fissures deepened, the chin lengthened and the stomach muscles swelled. The mirror at the other end of the room reproduced the phenomenon and you turned to follow it through the reflection, the ricochet of image.

He/they observed you. You saw in his/their eyes that he/they felt sleepy, a little cold and then, with no explanation, he/they disappeared through a slit in space. He/they existed, and then didn't; he/they had disappeared. The event didn't frighten you; you were quite familiar with that sort of magic.

What to do? You hadn't completed your task, Igal or Ilan or whoever it was had not listened to your advice. You studied the room. You felt a shadow, a breath, roaming around the room that caressed your face. Was it him/them? You saw the *Sefer ha-Malkuth;* you picked it up and leafed through the pages. You were tired, you felt a little cold. You stretched out your right arm and touched your belly. You wanted to speak but realized that your mission, your adventure, was over. You could now leave and make your trip to New York.

———

You walked down the stairs and tried to find your way out of the palace.

You had to talk with the squadron outside. The war had ended. You walked down a hall, entered a room, and went out the other door. You appeared on the esplanade. You saw, in front of you, a garden of burning bushes and mirrors rising up. How many? One or ten thousand. The dimension of that geography was limitless, eternal. It was a space that could be looked at ten thousand times. You saw a rabbit running quickly by, a rabbit with a watch tied around its neck. You walked on. You heard voices, howling, and suspected they came from the burning bushes. No, it was the peasants, the cadets, and the mercenaries, who were talking and smoking farther off. You were wonderstruck at the quantity of reflections. You didn't see yourself in the mirrors but you did see the bushes, the rabbit, and you saw photographs of your mother in Europe, during her imprisonment in a Nazi death camp, military hordes attacking an unknown bastion in Poland (at least you thought it was Poland), an onion, and a tenuous smile (just a smile, nothing else) on Amnon's lips.

From far away you saw the drawbridge. You crossed it. Outside there were soldiers waiting for you with rifles pointed up; then an unknown and vociferous colonel approached you. "Have you convinced him?"

"Yes and no, colonel." You summed it up for him. "Dalton is dead, Balkoff is dead and as far as I understand, there is nobody else in charge of the operation. To attack would produce a bloodbath. Convince the ones inside to give up, that's all."

"How do you know Igal Balkoff is dead?"

The question was a difficult one: "How?" you repeated. "It doesn't matter." You wanted to add something in English but you stopped cold. Better to say: "The true tragedy is what lies before you, colonel, based on the fact that the things of this world have no solution, and that moments of ecstasy are too few and escape like snowflakes under a hot sun. If you turn around and look up, you'll see the sun and its visual field will prevent you from admiring the misery that surrounds us. If, on the other hand, you look down, you'll see that we are evil beings, but you'll forget that perhaps hope exists above, toward the sun. Besides, it would be false to think that nature is intelligible, colonel. We embrace with too much insistence the idea of unity, of unidimensionality. The truth is that every rose is many roses, every individual many individuals, and every god many gods. We have been persuaded by Moses, the prophets, the rabbis, and the apostles, to believe in unity. A lie: the Egyptians, Aztecs, and Phoenicians were closer to reality with their polytheism than we are."

You were sure the colonel didn't understand you. You said goodbye on the sidewalk, all eyes following you. The colonel (you knew) was disillusioned with your undertaking; he would have liked other results. You walked on. Another shot sounded. You turned around, frightened, and the *Sefer ha-Malkuth* that you carried under your arm dropped through your hands. You kneeled down to retrieve it. It had been the colonel who had shot a bullet toward the infinite (toward G-d?). In that instant, a series of camera clicks were heard. That scene and its consequences would appear in tomorrow's newspapers.

———

You got into the limousine. Everything is a given but liberty exists anyway. The phrase echoed in your mind.

Where had you heard it? You remembered that Stabans had said it to you, while he amused himself telling you about various clinical cases discovered in a strange psychiatric manual that he found covered with dust in a library at the university, and that had been published around 1845. You opened the *Sefer ha-Malkuth* and saw that, in fact, the author of the manual was a Sir Walter Humprey Moor, native of Oxford. Why did your book have the capacity to name other authors and not its own?

One of the most exotic cases had been extracted in turn from another book, the *Mabul al ha-Yadaim*, published in Cairo in 1702 by Mir Bahadur Muhamma Alí. Walter Humprey Moor included it in his text and Stabans had recited it for you: A pious Muslim, Izadr, had been trying in vain to hide his shame. His problem consisted in knowing that his right hand did not possess the same will as the left. While the right one took coins from a hooded caftan that hung from a hook in the mosque as a loan, the other, just like in an adventure story, alarmed the crowd by raising a terrible racket, banging the table with a stick, striking it against the lectern, and throwing to the ground the books of our Lord, may his Blessed Memory be praised. The left hand acted in reaction to the right. Glances fell on the miserable

Muslim, Hasin ban Izadr. They accused him. What should he do? On another occasion the right hand, more affable although no more pacific than the other, robbed a bit of wax as it prepared candles for the fasting festival of Allah; it was surprised by the other that came down so hard on it with a machete that if it didn't slice three fingers off, it was only out of compassion of the Mighty Powerful. At the age of thirty the Muslim resorted to going to see the Dervish, who recommended that he wait until Pentecost Sunday and leave the problem to the will of the stars. If it rained the two nights before the Passover festival, it would be the sign to amputate the left hand. If it rained only one night, he must then cut off the right one. If he failed to do so, that would be evidence to Allah that the conflict could not be resolved in a personal manner, and then, when He wished it to be so, He would intervene. The Muslim was satisfied with the response and waited for the assigned day. Two weeks were left before the festival. He was anxious. When the day came, it rained two nights running. Following the instructions, Izadr took an axe, sharpened it, and with one slice, amputated his left hand. The right one eventually felt lonely, without company, and the sadness finally overcame it. It beat the chest of its owner in a sad, confessionary rhythm, and refused to respond to orders. In time, it accumulated so much energy that with one strike, it killed the Muslim himself.

Stavans, you remember, had told you that tale one rainy afternoon in Narvarte and gave as a final point this moral: while everything is a set, freedom is still attainable.

But what kind of freedom was it? The universe is predetermined (G-d knows beforehand our end), but free will exists. There are fixed rules and there is independence. Had you come to Paranagua out of free will, Talia, and out of free will would you leave? No, you were leaving bound, manipulated, trapped, with two tremendous responsibilities: the one of being a single mother and the other of educating a child without being sure of who you even were.

You flew to New York three days later. The flight lasted seven hours; you had cramps, there was turbulence, and the plane never quite straightened itself out.

You landed and they took you, Amnon, the lawyer Jeremías Seamslow, and your mother, to an apartment that your Uncle Harry, cousin of your dead father, had offered. It was luxurious, it had every technological comfort: heating, sauna, elevator operator, view of Central Park, but you couldn't care less about any of that (in spite of the fact that New York, in the past, had always fascinated you). It was deathly cold, the kind that seeped into your pores.

Your mother and the lawyer accompanied you to your physical at Mount Sinai; it lasted twenty-four hours in total. You kept the *Sefer ha-Malkuth* near you. You didn't care anymore how many copies existed, the important thing was that it always be at your side, especially while you went through these exams. It was your protection; it was your Judaism. Yes, the *Sefer ha-Malkuth* was *your* Judaism and *your* memory. You arrived at the lab on an empty stomach. By then your belly looked inflated and you would have to go the next day to buy maternity clothes. The doctors examined you from top to bottom; they did blood tests, X-rays, tapped you on the back and on the thighs to make sure your bones and clavicles were in place. They also applied a series of psychological tests. The pregnancy was normal, they said, although there was no predicting that the baby, after so many shocks, would be born sane and healthy.

Christmas was coming and the city was dressed for a party, with lights on its streets, music in the shops, clowns dressed as Santa Claus asking for donations for the poor, undocumented, and war veterans. What a change! The New York you saw from the taxi going from John F. Kennedy airport to Manhattan, or from the subway a few days later, looked ugly, feeble, pathological. The personal relationship one on one, person to person, did not exist for you, like in Paranagua, and you thought that the warmth of feeling had been substituted here for a constant rush, depersonalization, and the desire to make money. The shared social reality was a given, and nobody dared to question it, nobody dared to occupy the role of a Balkoff, to defy; the people were instead passive, a reproduction (without the intellectual, reflexive, or narrative talent) of Stavans. You had never had as many repellent epiphanies here. Even with its violence, its open inquietude, its nervous rhythm, you thought, New York could never imitate the absurd and frenzied Paranaguans, because that absurdness and frenzy had a special innocence, a something that touched you and moved you to nostalgia. In spite of the commemorative tone of the end of the year, the landscape bored you. Everything was so modern, so functional. As a response, you burrowed down into your bed and attempted to stay there for good.

You were depressed and your stability did not return. Would you ever recover your lost normality? Only time would give you the answer; you had to be patient. The life you had lived in the last eleven months had been radically transforming, aggressive, esoteric. You invoked, when you dozed in the mornings, intense images recently lived. You re-lived your acts, from your arrival in Tecamachalco until your farewell to the colonel in Aguaprieta. You saw the faces of the crowds, the weeping of Ofelia and Daniel at Liora's burial, you saw Stabans changing into Balkoff and vice versa, you remembered Dalton (you even recreated his final heroic gasps) and the cadets, Inés López Caballero, and you saw as well, more than one time in your memory, the starving man who appealed to you, in English, in the Paranaguan subway, saying: *I don't care if it rains or freezes, 'long as I have my plastic Jesus.* You felt, Talia, that Paranagua was inside you. You said to yourself: down with *love*, down with bourgeois *guilt*, down with *responsibility*. Up with masturbation—illegitimate copulation with space—up with polyphony.

You spent nights of insomnia and intense emotional swings, uncertainties, anguish. You had gone to Paranagua to look for a husband, and in your meditations there, you had resolved to return with empty hands, but never like this. You were a different person, you felt different, you walked, ate, bathed yourself, went to the bathroom, differently, as if another Talia had possessed your body. Was this maturity? Was this the adult universe? Your mother bought airline tickets for the trip back to Montreal but you resisted, you wanted to be alone, to saunter the noisy streets of New York, to lose yourself among the crowds, that in their turn were lost among the presents, the smiles, the hypocritical personalities. You were unenthusiastic; you were rude and disrespectful: Amnon tried to give you advice, he came into your room kindly, but you threw him out. One morning you were so dazed, you had spent such a bad night, tossing about in the sheets, listening to the night traffic, that, when provoked by your mother, you responded by throwing a plate at her with such force that you almost cut her in the head. How could you make your brief stay in Paranagua credible? You dreamed of total freedom, freedom from everything, everyone, freedom from yourself.

You got out of bed, you lay down again, you watched TV, absorbed and absent. The bed made you feel groggy and when you grew tired of it, you changed: you escaped before dawn, losing yourself in dark alleyways, sitting down to watch the eternal change of lights and colors in the street signals, or looking through the garbage for valuable objects. You went out without saying where you were going and would return at dusk, exhausted, breathless, clumsy, your clothes and the wool coat and your sweaty skin covered in dirt. You ate anything at all and never enough to satiate your appetite. You chewed on chicken bones, or fish, you chewed on apples, bananas, and gum like a ruminating cow, and (because a kind stranger gave you one) you began to drink beer. You also swallowed, between sips of beer, antidepressants, and they left you so exhausted that you fell asleep on sidewalks, in parks, or in bank entrances. I swore, when I saw you, that you were a beggar, an elegant woman, down on her luck, with the look of a timid, confused Madonna.

In all, you spent two weeks wandering around. The others were surprised by your deterioration: they had thought that in leaving Paranagua, everything could be resolved, but the opposite happened. You mother and

Amnon went to Montreal and then she came back temporarily. When will you stop persecuting me? you grumbled. She made appointments for you with more doctors and psychoanalysts, but you never went because you, Talia, wanted to live fully every single instant of that emotional collapse; you wanted to cultivate, to inhabit your depression, not to drive it away.

I thought: how much would I give for a crust of rye bread? The Sabbath was over and I was dressed in the caftan recently bought at Trumpeldor's, and the hat I wear on Rosh Hashana and Yom Kippur. My stomach growled; I hadn't found anything to eat and it was complaining. It was 3:45 p.m. I looked time and again at my watch.

Outside it was a typical December cold. Would I ever have a wife and children? Do imbeciles have the right to be happy? On Sabbath I rest, as God commands, and my turn to sweep the synagogue was scheduled for Sunday. It was 3:47. Sabbath had crept up on me and I had no time to make something to eat. The dining room at Keter Malkuth was closed and I felt guilty and ashamed because I was stained in G-d's eyes. I went out to walk along Madison; I had to kill the few minutes remaining before the service began to welcome in the new week. The orange of the afternoon gave way to the blue-green that comes with twilight, and the cars, fighting for their spots, pushed along in the traffic on the avenues. I gave myself as a goal in my journey the grocery of the shopkeeper Shmeruk (that, of course, would be closed). I walked. Absorbed in my meditations, watching on the ground the rhythm of the coming and going of the tips of my black patent leather shoes appearing and disappearing in front of me, I suddenly found myself looking right at Doctor Me'eman. He was at the door of the *mikva*. I walked toward him, stopped a few steps before, and looked at him: he is an old man, he has a curled beard that goes down to his navel and long greasy sidecurls that wrap around his ears. He asked me how I was, how I had spent the Sabbath. I nodded my head and didn't tell him that I was hungry, that I had forgotten to make myself something to eat. I didn't tell him because it would have been indiscreet.

"You're falling behind on your responsibilities, eh?"

Why had he said that? Had my appetite revealed itself in my eyes?

"I read the *Torah*, Dr. Me'eman, and . . ."

"And? Do you understand any of it?"

Why was he looking at me with such distrust? Of course I understood the *Torah* and he knew it. I had been a student at our yeshiva, I had written a composition for him. It must be my hunger that was ravaging my spirit, and his as well.

"I want a wife," I said to him.

"To every man there is apportioned one woman, and only one. The couple is like a circle: it is made of two complementary half moons. You must wait, Lifeshit. You must wait for your other half. But you are not an olive, have patience. The messiah, we know, could arrive any minute."

"Yes," I obligingly affirmed.

"Besides," he went on, "you didn't take advantage of your opportunity with Reizel, you know very well. The dowry was paid. We had spoken with Reb Haim and had made an agreement. She would be coming from Istanbul where she had spent the last year working for a charity organization. The ceremony was ready, the dowry, the rabbi, the mikva, but you called it off."

"I didn't feel anything for her."

"People learn to love each other."

"She was silly."

"Who were you to judge her, Lifeshit? Only G-d can judge."

"I saw her and I was disappointed. She chewed with her mouth open. I want someone exciting, who knows how to think."

"Someone who thinks for you, that's what you want, no?"

I laughed like a fool. The doctor likes it when I act demented. We spoke later about this "someone exciting." He complained that I read too many adventure novels, that I wanted my ideal wife to be a CIA spy, or an envoy from Israel on an impossible mission to Egypt or Jordan. Your mind is on Jupiter, Lifeshit, he told me. No, I said, I'll make do with someone more immediate, a daring woman, who comments and searches. The doctor laughed: a daring woman doesn't care about keeping house, he added, she isn't fertile, or if she is, she is a whore, and the Mishnah prohibits that type of casual sex. We changed the subject. Dr. Me'eman wanted to know if I had completed my punishment: staying in my room, with no milkshakes or novels or jam, for three days, for having lost the envelopes that Nuchem gave me for the congregation. I responded affirmatively and told him that I had spent the sentence by candlelight, imagining a story where the protagonist (myself, in this case) was a strawberry milkshake. He thought I was making fun of him and he got angry. He said nothing more and he left. It was 4:10.

I felt confused. I kept on walking toward Shmeruk's store. I listened to the city noises, thinking about Borges's poems dedicated to Israel in 1967, to Spinoza and to the golem. I soon turned on 54th Street and it was then that I saw the young woman hiding behind a post. She had a big, beautiful book under her arm, and she protected it in the warmth of her coat. What did her face look like? I don't know, I'll never know. She was dirty, pale, ragged. Her mouth opened and closed like a ferocious tiger.

It was Talia. She walked over to me slowly, doubtingly. She was ashamed but soon recuperated and began to talk. "You're one of those orthodox Jews, right?" she asked me. "A crow."

I didn't know what to say. Why was she talking to me? She went on: I've seen them in Manhattan, at the jewelry stores on 47th Street."

"My name is Lifeshit and I'm hungry. The Sabbath will be over soon and I'll eat a crust of rye bread," I responded. She was aggressive, spiny.

"Why do your sidecurls hang like that? Have you ever heard of a barber shop? Your sect . . ."

"Keter Malkuth."

"Keter Malkuth. Do they accept new members?"

What could I say? I ignored her and kept walking. It was 4:25. Why should I let myself be entwined in Satan's claws? Women have the devil inside them, that is what Dr. Me'eman says. Talia looked at me candidly, she devoured me with her eyes. I tried to ignore her but I couldn't and I turned around. I saw her: angelic, sweet, dressed in a white corset and a silk tunic. How had she changed clothes so quickly? She looked like a celestial being, a dream. She held a bow in her left hand, or an ancient weapon, and in her right hand she held the book. Her legs were crossed and she was looking at her toenails. She was barefoot, there in the cold.

"You look like Venus de Milo. Why do you have . . ." I started to ask.

"I could be yours, Lifeshit. I am . . . Do you know how I'm going to name the son I'm carrying inside me? Igal, Igal Stavans."

"Stavans?"

"Igal Stabans."

"I don't understand."

"Synonym of the other, Igal Balkoff."

"I don't know what you're talking about, but I'm not an idiot."

Her next words were in Spanish. She told me to read well the story of Talia (her story) and her enmity with heaven. She talked about the Stabanses, about Liora, Daniel and Ofelia Stabans, of Balkoff, Dr. Jekyll, Mr. Edward Hyde, and of Dorian Gray. "Who are they?" I asked. "Where are they from? I don't think I know them. Where did you learn Spanish? You have a Paranaguan accent."

"Paranaguan . . ."

"I'm from Paranagua, too. I lived there until they brought me to New York, to stay with some cousins, to help the Keter Malkuth congregation."

"Keter Malkuth, just like the name of my book." She showed me the book she was carrying. It was called *Sefer ha-Malkuth*. I had never seen it before. Days later I asked Dr. Me'eman if he knew of the book, and he told me that one Calman Schultz, a Polish writer, author of *The Encyclopedia of the Dead* and *Hourglass*, world famous in the twenties, had promised to write a book of that name. He lived in Drogobych and in 1943, a Nazi, to prove his bravery, had killed him in the street. As he died, Schultz held the manuscript under his arm and protected it with pride. But the text vanished. Up to this day, its location was unknown and thought to have been burned.

"So—what could be better, Lifeshit? You must possess me, I will be yours if you want. Isn't Paranagua a magical and exotic place?"

"Who said so?"

I felt my stomach shrinking and stretching. My hunger was wreaking havoc inside me. It was 4:45.

"I'm hungry."

"You are too worried about your stomach."

"How do you know?"

"I know."

It was true: nothing was more important, more essential to me, than to eat. How did she know? I was silent and Talia went on: "There are those who deny misery by pointing toward the sun, and those who negate the sun by fixing instead on misery."

I laughed. What was she trying to say to me?

"It's true, believe me. You and I are man and wife."

I had to go back, I had to talk to Dr. Me'eman. I remembered the words: You're letting your responsibilities go, eh Lifeshit? I ran quickly back to my room and left the girl behind. My footsteps beat stiffly against the pavement. I changed clothes again, put on the old caftan and a different yarmulke. It was 5:10. What had I done during the last hour? Why were the seconds so quickly disappearing? I entered the synagogue.

I walked out during the prayers. Nuchem and Reb Chaim Kopikis looked at me angrily; Dr. Me'eman didn't know I had left. What cold! Would Talia still be on the corner of Madison Avenue? I ran to look for her. My stomach was, more than ever, a yawning, groaning space. It was 7:35. I would have given my kingdom for a crust of rye bread!

She wasn't on Madison, or on 54th Street either. The post was still there, alone, hiding no one. When I got to Lexington Avenue, I saw her from afar. She held the *Sefer ha-Malkuth* in her arms and she kissed it as she chewed on an apple and a piece of bread. She had her back to me and couldn't see me. I did everything I could to catch up to her but she turned down an alley and dissolved like a ghost. I looked for her, but nothing. I felt that the world was mocking me and that I had wasted another opportunity.

Talia touched me like we are touched by the morning. I returned to Keter Malkuth (the congregants were coming out of the service), went to the dining room, ate a yogurt, went to my room and fell asleep. In vain I have tried to remember what she looked like. Who were you, Talia? Eighteen times Adonai's bride.

TRANSLATED BY AMY PRINCE

The Spot

Better to get used to it. After all, what's a spot? No big deal: a nuisance, something trivial. I left the house that morning like any other morning, in a rush and worried about the same old things. Carpe diem, I'm sure I said. I had to be in school in less than an hour. A bus and train ride awaited me. I remember selecting the shirt. (Or had it been waiting for me in the closet?) I shaved, put my belt and tie on the bed. The phone rang but I didn't answer. Although it was already with me, I ignored it out of distraction as we do the most urgent matters, the ones that sooner or later make our lives unbearable and force us to send everything to hell. I was still in the elevator, just after arriving at school, when I saw the cloudy spot, dark and oily, on the front of my shirt's white vastness, just under the right shoulder. The first thing I did was to see if anyone, some busybody, had already seen it, but luckily no one had. I touched it softly with my fingertip, feeling resigned and overcome by an uneasiness I couldn't shake off. Truth was I would've liked to rip it off, snuff out its hateful existence, but I chose to be polite. I was in the elevator and had to put on an act in front of the others. Since when have you been there, bitch? I couldn't remember the exact awful moment it entered this world, stamping itself on me without an invitation. Had a car splashed me mid-block? Or had it been a screaming boy in the subway car? Why hadn't the Chinese Laundromat seen it? An unforgivable mistake. I'd have to find a better cleaner. But for now what was the solution? Make it disappear, erase it. Not so easy. I had to find one of those magic potions advertised on TV that clean without leaving a trace. Go to a supermarket, but how? Class began in twenty minutes. Anyway, there was no store nearby. My sense of anger and lunacy grew by the minute. Ignore it. Then I thought about all the filthy, dirty people, in particular, those men who come back from the john with an apple-sized spot by the zipper, as if the last drop had broken its course. I also thought of a fat woman cheerfully coming out of a restaurant with a spot under the chin where the defiant forkful hadn't made it down the gullet. Sooner or later, we all get spots, I told myself. They are part and parcel of life. What is a cloud if not a spot? And what's a shadow? But students, colleagues, the secretary, the whole world would notice. What a shame! That's life: you shower, you get dressed pretending there's order in the world, that your body and clothes are clean, then, all of a sudden, an indication of filth, of. . . . Lowering my shoulder, I stepped out of the elevator. I recalled that several months ago, a lady sitting in front of me with a shopping bag in a packed bus told me as she rang the buzzer to get out: "Excuse me sir, but your zipper . . . ugh, how can I put it? Really, you should know your fly is down and well . . . You know what the world is like now." I felt the sky crashing down upon me and that my throbbing heart, beating rapid-fire, was more than I could take. I felt—what did I feel? I realized I had four options: despite the awful heat, I could wear the sweater in my office drawer and pretend I had a cold and that my doctor had suggested I wear it, or else keep my hand tucked like Napoleon Bonaparte for the rest of the day or just turn half way around and quickly tell the secretary that I wouldn't be in class, to make up any sort of excuse. The last option, sheer lunacy, was to take some scissors, but damn, the shirt had cost me an arm and a leg and I had only worn it twice. I went straight to the bathroom. I took off my shirt one, two, three, soaked the spotted edge in cold water, then stretched it flat. How stupid of me! The whole area was shadowed by a huge cloud. This is when my paranoia got the best of me. I couldn't leave the bathroom because the spot was even more noticeable. On the other hand, staying there, stubbornly closed in, was the mark of an unstable mind. A spot. What's in a spot? My colleagues—what would they think? They'd come in to take a piss and comb their hair, they'd see me and ask if I was okay. I had no choice but to stay like this until . . . I suddenly understood how a tiny problem had grown beyond my control. A spot, an omen, a huge and awful reality. Fear. What if someone had arranged for this awful, filthy spot to throw me to the bottom of the well of confusion? And if it were the beginning of the end? I had lost my freedom. I was imprisoned. Yes, a hateful group of enemies had planned this misadventure. The spot was my punishment. The spot. Tomorrow a detective would find my body and the forensic doctor would say that not only my clothes, but all my skin, even the pores were covered with . . . The autopsy, the cause of death, a total mystery. No, no, no, nooooooo. I couldn't just give up, no way. With my spirit torn to shreds, I bravely decided to put my shirt back on. The spot was still there but the water had . . . I lowered my eyes. I saw, not without a good bit of shock, that my pants were now full of spots and that . . . It had all begun with a meaningless . . . A spot, a zipper. A . . . I tried to convince myself, nobody has died of . . . But under my chin, another dark spot. Another and another and . . . I wanted to get used to it. After all, a spot is nothing more than a slight inconvenience. At wit's end, I went into a bathroom stall and wrapped toilet paper around my throat. Then I stuck my head, my carefully shaven face, my hair so meticulously combed since morning, in the john and that was the end of all spots and all shame. To hell with carpe diem. . . . Pssshhhh and the phone.

⌐══⌐

TRANSLATED BY ALISON STAVCHANSKY AND DAVID UNGER

HOUSE REPOSSESSED

Body and soul must be cured together, as head and eyes . . .
ROBERT BURTON, *THE ANATOMY OF MELANCHOLY*

AS A GIRL, WHENEVER MY MOTHER SAID, "YOU KNOW YOU RESEMBLE YOUR uncle. . . ," I would immediately feel a vibration. And, by sheer magic, I would invoke the labyrinthine house, which I had imagined from multiple perspectives but was never allowed to visit. The invocation made me feel happy, very happy, as if I had once inhabited the house myself but had been pushed out, with Irene and Jules, when it was taken over.

The vibration disappeared and then, shortly after I got over my painful divorce, it resumed again. Looking back, I realized I had not experienced it for years. Certainly more than a decade. I had forgotten its sour-sweet aftershocks, its pleasure and fury intertwined.

It would always begin. . . . It would begin as an eerie sensation. The strange, unspeakable sensation of a tiny, porcelain-like ant climbing up my left leg until getting lost amongst my pubic hair. A parasite crawling inside my body. Almost simultaneously, I would feel a rough cheek passionately caressing my breasts. Then the ant would inhabit my vagina, twisting and staggering and jolting and arching.

161

My uncles abandoned the house sometime around 1950. They had been born there, and so had my mother. The house had been the family's property for generations. People would say that its old, spacious rooms smelled of ancient memories. You could sense the presence of relatives in every dusty corner.

I was three years old when Uncle Jules left the country. I had seen his picture in newspapers, in the back jacket of many books. But I didn't remember him as a presence. And yet, I would often dream about him. Frightening dreams. I would wake up sweaty and badly shaken. He would appear in a dark, overused jacket, with his long, unruly beard, smoking his cigarette, always laughing. He would point down at the floor—to what seemed to me to be a sewer. And he would tell me that I had not yet done what I promised I would do. I never promised him anything. Although perhaps I did.

My mother kept the whole affair of the house to herself. A family secret. I soon realized it was hard for her to talk about it. Only slowly, in a fragmentary fashion, she would let things go. She had never kept a healthy relationship with Irene and Jules. And she left the house early on, still in her teens. So she preferred to change the subject every time I asked. But I pressed her because I wanted to know more. I wanted to know every detail, every bit of information. Deep inside I felt that the house had always been mine. As if I was part of a long chain of generations and sooner or later I would be called to reclaim my lost property.

The ant . . . My immediate reaction would be to salivate. My underpants would get wet and an unusual, irregular heat, a passionate heat, would follow.

The whole thing, salivation and heat and passion, could occur in the middle of the night. But it also happened in the middle of the day. The rough cheek would possess me. It wasn't like making love with my ex-husband. Something more profound and painful. As if a child had been incubated in me. The child of an ant. As a result, I would be confused. Totally confused. I would be ready to scream. But what for?

I remember when I first saw the house from afar. I must have been six or seven. My mother and I, I think we were on our way to the grocery store, walking on Rodríguez Peña. I suddenly sensed a strange silence in her. The vibration, did I feel it that day? We stopped and she looked up. "A horrible house . . . ," she uttered. "Irene and Jules used to live here."

She added very little. Something about my aunt spending her entire life knitting on the bedroom sofa. And about her dying after Uncle Jules moved to Europe. "Hers was a slow death," my mother said. "She had to work on it two or three years. Nostalgia and the absence of companionship . . . She paid the price." At the moment of death my mother was next to Irene. But she nurtured a deep filial hatred toward her. One day she told me, "Your uncles, they behaved liked a married couple."

I remember asking her if we could go in. "Impossible. No one can get in." I asked who lived there. "Nobody lives inside. Empty. It's always empty. And it will always be."

I now wonder if every time I passed in front of the house, I would feel a vibration. Perhaps. As a little girl, I didn't pay much attention to it because . . . because I thought it was normal. Or at least I think I did.

I have read, time and again, Uncle Jules's diary of the loss of the house. It's curious the way he predicted that one day I would reenter it. He surely loved the place. No doubt about it. He loved it from beginning to end. "Irene and I would die here someday," he wrote. "Obscure and distant cousins would inherit the place, have it torn down, sell the bricks, and get rich on the building plot."

His description of the layout is quite graphic: the dining room, a living room with tapestries, the library, and three large rooms. A corridor separated that section from the front wing, where there was a bath, the kitchen, Julia and Irene's bedrooms, and the hall. He makes a written map so that others can begin to understand the siege under which both he and Irene lived.

He also writes in his diary that the forced evacuation happened without much fuss. He began hearing noises in the library and in the dining room. Soon after, entrance to those sections of the house was prohibited. He constantly writes about a "They." "I had to shut the door to the passage," he writes, "because they have taken over the back part." To which Irene, calmly and without remorse, would reply: "From now on we'll have to live on this side."

Uncle Jules wouldn't show any fear. "Aside from our nocturnal rumblings," he writes, "everything was quiet in the house. During the day there were the household sounds, the metallic click of knitting needles, the rustle of stamp-album pages turning."

Days before I had the strongest vibration of all, a photograph of the house appeared in the newspaper. A murder on Rodríguez Peña, a couple of yards away. The reporter accompanied his text with a picture, which I studied carefully.

Nothing had changed. It remained just as I remembered it. I called my mother. She didn't want to talk about it. But she did say a postcard from Uncle Jules had arrived from Marseilles. The first one in decades because I don't remember ever seeing his handwriting. He didn't say anything in particular. Just that he had been traveling with a girlfriend to and from Paris, and was overwhelmed by the thought of his distant family in the southern cone.

Distant family.

When I heard about the postcard, the vibrations increased. And then, they immediately ceased.

But now I knew that the ant, shaking and revolving, had remained inside me and would not vanish.

The ant . . .

I kept the whole thing to myself. At least for a while. Until the next night, when I think I called my mother. I was determined to explain to her the bizarre feelings I was having. But the moment we got on the phone, I couldn't. Was unable to. Instead, I asked her more about the postcard and about the house and about Uncle Jules and Aunt Irene.

I don't remember what she answered. That's precisely the time when I stopped paying attention. Within minutes I found myself en route to the house once taken over. As I walked, the vibration appeared again, less intense.

My left leg felt numb. I was affected by a high fever and felt terribly sick. Terribly sick.

But I didn't stop walking.

I stopped three or four blocks away from the place, to catch my breath. Then I resumed walking and found myself right in front of its main door.

I remember Uncle Jules's description of how one enters the house through a vestibule with enameled tiles, beyond which a wrought-iron grated door opens onto the living room.

I stood immobilized. Should I enter or shouldn't I? It had been empty for decades. I looked around suspiciously and saw, to my surprise, a sewer.

I didn't have a key to the house. Was there ever one? I pushed the entrance door and the lock, too rusty, fell apart. Just as in a gothic tale one reads in high school, the door opened, making a macabre noise. Although, now that I think of it, perhaps somebody opened it. Somebody's hand.

Darkness, silence. A feeling of liberation and then again, imprisonment. The rough, indelicate cheek . . . Its fingers were . . . I was being penetrated.

I thought of Irene and Jules. They would complain of terrible boredom because nothing worthwhile would happen in Buenos Aires. And yet, their life was quite pleasurable. At least until they were forced out of the house.

I felt ashamed, overwhelmed by the kind of shame a child feels after a parent points out a stupid mistake. My mother had forbidden me to enter this house. And yet, here I was, entering. Or better, being entered by the house.

I began hearing voices. I knew Irene used to walk in her sleep. That would wake Uncle Jules up and keep him awake all night.

"It's not here."

"Yes."

"You're sure?"

"I know I am."

I wanted to turn around and leave. But I couldn't. I knew I couldn't. The ant was moving inside me. Obsessively. Consistently. Without compassion. I was provoking and was being provoked. My vagina . . . I imaged a map to my vagina: a large empty box with tapestries, a cold corridor with the ant at its end.

My breath accelerated.

I couldn't. . . . I wanted to stop but I couldn't. Yes, I wanted to stop.

"I'm knitting . . ."

"You look tired."

"In that case, we'll have to live on this side."

"Look at the pattern I just figured out. Doesn't it look like a four-leaf clover? Or like a tropical tree?

"No tropical trees around here. You know that, my dear."

I was shaking. I turned around and abruptly found myself lying on the floor. A glimmering light appeared in what I thought was the dining room. At a far distance I saw a woman relaxed on a sofa. Soon after, as the wrought-iron grated door opened, I saw a lofty figure. Probably a man. Yes, a man, very tall and thin. "You know you resemble your uncle . . . ," I heard my mother whispering in my ear. "You really do look alike."

Again, a voice. "They've taken over our section, too."

The man moved toward me. A long beard, a cigarette. Uncle Jules. It was Uncle Jules. He was laughing. "Yes," he said. "Yes. And I didn't have

time to bring much. We had what we had and that was it. I even remembered 15,000 pesos in my bedroom wardrobe. But it was too late. I had to
leave. The whole country was possessed. You know that, don't you? I only
had my wrist watch on, so I felt terrible."

He pointed toward a window. "I locked the front door up tight and tossed
the key down the sewer. It wouldn't do to have some poor devil decide to
go in, would it? But I'm proud to say I have recovered it."

I felt very angry. Angry and annoyed. I hated him. I hated Uncle Jules.
Actually, I realized I had hated him since I was a little girl. Silently. I closed
my eyes and with an agile move, touched my pubic hair.

I began to masturbate. It wasn't that I wanted pleasure. No, not the least.
I had decided to extirpate the ant and fight the rough cheek persecuting me.
To get them out of and away from my system as soon as possible.

Sitting alone on the cold floor, surrounded by darkness, my fingers
moved diligently.

In ecstasy, I said to myself: "They liked the house, Irene and Jules."

Yes, we like the house. And as I raised my head, I realized that, after a
difficult struggle, I had finally caught the ant and could now squeeze it if I
wanted to. I smiled happily, stood up and walked toward the door. Not far
from it, in a dusty corner, I found its lost key.

Our key.

TRANSLATED BY THE AUTHOR

Three Nightmares

To remember Betzi is to invoke three nightmares, with their interludes. None of them give enough details about our relationship, I know. Perhaps they even hide its significance. The truth is that I don't understand details either. Living with Betzi was a way of functioning for me. While we were together, her kisses and caresses would awaken delightful feelings. I would turn over my realm if I could prolong them. But then came the shower of disagreements. We shouted at each other, cursed at each other, contradicted each other, and everything turned into chaos. I stopped understanding. Today I'm cured of the caresses, but not of the dreams.

It all started when I irresponsibly lost my wedding ring. It was a plain gold ring. We had bought it at a small, cramped downtown jewelry store. I couldn't remember when and where I misplaced it. In the office? During lunch? I looked for it until I was exhausted and returned home feeling ashamed, with the intention of explaining to Betzi what had happened. She was furious and let out a scream as big as the world. I apologized. What could I do? While I did promise to look for it better, I never thought the incident could have such connotations. Well, the first nightmare occurred the following night, after an exciting game of poker. Several friends of mine and I had gathered together at home. We bought whiskey, tequila, and appetizers that the maid improved with cheese, onions, and dip. We drank quite a bit. It was after midnight. Betzi had arrived home late from the office and in a bad mood. She seemed to have springs in her face and a grumpy, stony grimace. The alcohol was starting to go to my head. I was dizzy and had the vague sensation that I was drowning in a fish tank. Packs of cards would go. Come back. Noise. The piercing rattling of two bottles that would shatter. Cigarette smoke. I wanted to vomit and, excusing myself, ran to the bathroom and locked myself in for fifteen minutes. For exactly fifteen minutes I threw up my stomach. The light bulb over the mirror hurt my eyes. I felt chills. Betzi was shouting at me, saying, "Are you all right, Messeguer?" "Yes," I replied, feeling embarrassed. (Now that I think about it, I know that Betzi controlled me like a witch.) Later on she knocked on the door. I opened it; she looked at me and ran into the dining room where my friends were. "Someone go to the drug store," she said. "I need a bottle of milk of magnesia for Messeguer. . . ." How embarrassing! Getting drunk is one of the hardest challenges a man can undergo . . . and I had failed. How long had it been since I last drank? Long enough to lose my resistance . . . to become a child again. To be honest, I would have wanted to vomit my discomfort at Betzi. A shower wouldn't have done me any harm, but I didn't even manage to open the faucet. I waited for Betzi to come and cure me. I later came out of the bathroom and collapsed on the sofa. My friends disappeared. Had the game ended? In my cotton-filled eardrums the voices sounded like squeaking rats, like rusty locks. That was when I had the nightmare that woke me in a single bound. Hours had gone by. Betzi was in the bedroom. I walked up the stairs. The room was dark. Depressed, I slipped into bed between the sheets. "Very quiet, aren't you?" she stammered. My heart trembled. "Arrhythmia," I replied. "My lungs hurt. My heart beats too fast. It was

those appetizers that the maid served. They provoked a horrible nightmare."
She turned the lamp on. "Talk to me," she said. I resisted. "Relax . . . now,
now . . . ," she said, soothing me. "You're nervous. You lost your rhythm.
What happened?" Then I told her the sequence of the dream: I was in a
grayish room, with very high walls, frozen. Actually, it wasn't a room but a
warehouse. Or a refrigerator. One of those old refrigerators that smell damp
because the owner forgot to clean it. I felt I was suffocating. I looked for
some window or door, an area in which I could breathe. Nothing. Why was
I encased in that box? In the center of the box there was a wooden bench.
Should I sit down? I walked around in circles, without direction, like a madman. I walked around the bench. Suddenly, a uniformed guard, wearing
gloves, a helmet with a visor, and boots, appeared at the corner. His pupils
followed the outline of my heels, the joints of my knees. One, two . . . One,
two . . . One, two . . . Absurd situation. One, two . . . One, two . . . I would
approach him, but he would back away. Surely he was prohibited to mingle
with the prisoners. With gloves on, his hands held up his belt . . . or perhaps
his belt held up his hands. He had a hairy, curved mustache. "Listen," I told
him. But he would ignore me. Nearby, I discovered a briefcase. It was inex-
pensive, conventional, and Italian-made, with a greenish-yellow band on the
side. Surely it hadn't been there before. I was intrigued by its contents. But
before I even had the chance to approach it, an abominable monster, a strange
medusa, sprang out of its interior. Transparent, it had a dozen tentacles on
each side of its body, and wore jewelry. Pearls and rings with diamonds, hindu
gems and rubies were hanging from its nose, ears, and long hair. But it wasn't
hair that flourished on its head: it was cables, miles of multicolored cables
of different calibre. A mouldy, rotten, and ridiculous-looking sight. Its long,
blackish eyelashes were surrounded by electric bulbs. It was a mechanical
medusa that vomited (like me in the bathroom), not stomach residue, but
semen. It spit semen when it spoke while its tentacles oscillated happily, to
and fro, contracting like worms. "Benito Messeguer, we've decided on your

sentence." He was saying my name, which implied that he knew who I was. "You have one week to present three letters of recommendation." Three letters? Why? Addressed to whom? "Messeguer, think about what I'm saying. This isn't a joke. Your life is in danger. You lost that ring and deserve the worst punishments. We want to help you. We want you to bring those letters. Through those letters we can prove that you deserve to go on living interminably . . . to continue being Benito Messeguer . . . Understand?" No, I didn't understand. I hadn't even realized the connection between the refrigerator and the ring. "This is a nightmare. Do you know what a nightmare is? We receive reports of bad behavior. You're just like everyone else, Messeguer, and then some. We won't allow serious depravity. Would you like to continue being Benito Messeguer? Very well then . . . , commit yourself!" I was confused. What were they blaming me of? "It's advisable that you not be too clever. People like you deserve to be in the sewers, crawling like reptiles. We're going to give you a little pat on the rear." I was looking at the guard out of the corner of my eye, who until then had been daydreaming and who now, obligingly, applauded his bosses' words. "I warn you, Messeguer, refusing won't do you any good. We have spies placed in strategic areas. They're following your every move. They know what your mind knows." I felt dizzy and replied: "I don't plan to cooperate." The medusa was becoming furious. "Messeguer, please! Know that by not cooperating, you'll be helping us even more. Remember: three letters of recommendation in one week. Come now, my friend, wake up. The week has just begun."

Betzi burst out laughing. She was making fun of me and her smile was terrifying. "They'll kill you," she announced. "You don't even know under what pretext you should ask for those letters of recommendation. You're screwed, Messeguer!" And as she said this, tears of laughter trickled down her face. "But . . . in case they do kill you," she then said with dignity, "make sure they do it in the most delicate way possible." "What are you talking about?" I asked. "Have you gone crazy? You seem to be spying for them."

And Betzi continued: "That's your punishment for having lost the ring." The discussion and Betzi were both proving to be detestable. Still, she gave herself the luxury of finishing, by saying: "What a pity, Benito! You would be better off dead." I felt an unprecedented rage. "Shut up," I said. "Shut up. You're going to destroy me. You're a witch. Please, leave me alone." I left the room, slamming the door behind me. I wanted to kill her.

In the days that followed I found myself driving away ghosts that perch themselves on my knees and shadows that attack me. (I know ghosts don't exist, that's why I would drive them away.) I felt like brutalizing someone, like losing control. There exists resistant men who know how to love . . . and others who are weaker, and dwarfish, who are trapped by passion. My love for Betzi was the trustworthy mirror of my inabilities and fears. Similar were the days that went by during which she acted more and more strangely. She would get up from eating breakfast without giving me my customary good-bye kiss. And she would get into her heavy fox fur coat, and would put perfume on while she frowned, loathsome—yes, ignoring me. Hurt and very sad, I would lock myself in the bathroom for more than fifteen minutes and wouldn't come out even if the telephone rang. Or I would shave for hours. I even stopped going to work. If they would call from the office, I wouldn't come to the phone. And what if the maid was a spy?, I would ask myself. Everything was in a state of confusion. At noon, Betzi would also call. She would ask if the gas tank was full or if the bed clothes were being aired out . . . and only at the end, when she was about to hang up, would she ask about me. One time I answered her phone call, saying: "Why didn't you say goodbye?" She replied with whatever stupidity, and then again I said: "What do you think they'll do to me, Betzi, if I don't turn in those letters of recommendation?" "Messeguer, you're an imbecile," she replied, and then she cut me off. She had called me an imbecile.

My mind started to plan requests, think of relatives or close friends from whom I could ask for letters of recommendation. I had to look for someone who knew me well, who had confidence in me. I thought about my poker friends, my boss at the office, my brother. And what was I going to tell them? They would think that I had lost my mind. (Had I?) What do you need to prove, Messeguer? they would ask.

One morning I got on the route number 5 bus, the same bus that would take me to the office every morning. It was horrible. The passengers were watching me. They looked like spies who were working for the medusa. A little girl kept looking at my hands, while her mother had her attention focused on my zipper. (For a moment I thought it was open, but no.) Another individual wearing a silly tie was bending his mouth downward. He felt sorry for me. Even the bus driver, when I went to pay him, waved away the change. He avoided touching me. "Go away!" I shouted, without holding myself back any longer. An old woman tried to help me, but I pushed her. I got off the bus and stumbled into a concrete median. I had a headache and I was exhausted. I returned home and the maid had to open the door for me because I couldn't find the key. She looked at me with fearful eyes. It's funny: hanging from a handle in her right hand was a suitcase. I could have sworn that it was the medusa's briefcase. "Ms. Betzi called," she said. "She's had to leave for Rochester. It's a *ternational* conference." I deduced that *ternational* meant international. Ternational: the word sounded nice. Betzi was a fashion designer. She designed winter dresses, belts, and shoes. Her professional commitments would call for her to travel frequently, go away. I understood the message. I understood that international conferences could be improvised. What was the maid doing with that suitcase? "Where did you get it," I asked her. "She'll be in Rochester for two days. Said the lady who owned an inn . . ." She mechanically repeated the same phrase. "That's not what I asked you," I said. "Where did you get that suitcase?" "Which suitcase?" she replied. The maid's hands were empty. I had been dreaming. My throat was dry. "What's the matter, Mr. Messeguer?" she asked. I had been a normal guy until the day before yesterday, and now I was lowering my guard. A bit later I took two aspirin. I also took an antibiotic capsule remaining in the medicine chest and lay down to sleep.

My brother called that afternoon. "Benito, why aren't you at the office?" he said. "As a favor, I need a letter of recommendation from you," I told him. "I'm ceasing to be who I am," and I disclosed my critical moments, the hallucinations. "You've lost your mind, dear. It's Betzi, she's bewitching you." I got on the defensive: "No, she's innocent. It's the mid-life crisis. I'm afraid . . ." "Stop worrying. Separate yourself from that woman, I know what I'm telling you. You've never been so frail. You had a reputation for being responsible. Stop worrying! People die of typhoid, cancer . . . but never from having had a nightmare . . . and even less, from owing three letters of recommendation." He laughed. The conversation was encouraging. One word echoed in my mind: *frail . . . frail.* I hung up the receiver and immediately felt better. It's the convalescence of my soul, I thought. I should recover. Your brother is right: you're afraid of Betzi. She's bewitched you. That innermost dissatisfaction is creating this sequence of apparitions. . . . You should alleviate your anxiety.

Another three days went by without Betzi, without controlling my patience, without logic. Three absurd days. I kept looking for the ring. I cleaned the office, and the basement of the house—where I had repaired a pruning hook, looking for the damned ring. And I had a few classified ads placed in the newspaper *Excélsior*. Nothing. That's when I decided to buy another ring. It's necessary, I told myself. Its importance hid powerful secrets. Replacing it would return some lost happiness to me. I went to the same downtown jewelry store and explained to the salesman exactly what I wanted: a plain ring, not luxurious, although made of gold, to replace the previous one. Although they had discontinued the style, they could match it by request. The replacement would be more expensive and they couldn't assure me it was going to be identical. "However . . . nothing is identical," said the salesman. "Things look like themselves." Yes, there would be a similarity, but it would also have its own qualities. After much talk, I accepted. It would be ready in two weeks: the gold would be melted down, and the original mold would have to be found. That would take several days. They would have to work very carefully. No, my urgency was too great. He should have it ready by the end of the week, the date of the second nightmare. The salesman said that he would try, though he couldn't promise. This was enough reason to make me happy. I returned home. There was no news from Betzi, not even a telegram. I thought about the possibility of having been deceived for years during my marriage. While she provoked this emotional crisis, she surely had another man inserted between her legs. All women are bitches, I thought. They're all witches. I wanted to get revenge, to avenge myself somehow. I walked around in the bedroom, went up the stairs, down, and walked around in circles like a madman.

⁘⸻⸗

The seventh day arrived and the jewelry store didn't have the ring ready. I was exhausted. Even so, I did everything possible not to fall asleep. No, I didn't want to. I resisted, but in the end . . . I dropped off. In front of me was the same refrigerator. The same guard with the belt holding up his hands. The same visor. I was sitting on that bench. In the farthest corner was the briefcase radiating heat. Hours would go by . . . and nothing. Surely they've forgotten about me, I thought. They must be busy reading other letters of recommendation . . . or dreaming them. Suddenly the guard approached me: "Congratulations. We know that you haven't obtained a single letter." Why was he congratulating me? Immediately the transparent medusa appeared out of the briefcase. Its cables were coiled and dirty with grease. It looked like a bubbling sea sponge. "Stop worrying," it was telling me. "Luckily, we've found your ring. You left it here." What? That's impossible. "I misplaced it two or three days before coming here. You couldn't have found it." "Don't be clever, Messeguer. If I tell you we found the ring . . . it's because we found the ring. Look at it." He extended one of its tentacles, showing me the ring amongst so much other jewelry. "Take it, Messeguer, and be attentive. It would displease us very much if we had to judge you again," it was saying while it gave it to me. I slipped it onto the knuckle of my left pinkie finger. "Be happy!" said the medusa, in conclusion. "This nightmare has also ended."

What? I woke up drenched in sweat. I had been used like a puppet. I had never lost the ring, nor did I ever have it. Everything was in a state of confusion. I examined my hand, and there it was. What a surprise! My heart was beating at a wicked pace. Suddenly, I fell asleep again, thus allowing the final nightmare to begin. The following was its sequence: I'm on a shadowy street, standing feverishly under the light of a lamppost, and smoking. I'm wearing a gray suit and preparing to go to the movies. I know that they're showing the film *Shanghai Express* with Marlene Dietrich one or two blocks away. I arrive at the ticket booth and find a beautiful, robust woman there. She's lost her ticket. I want to help her but my shyness impedes me. Immediately she asks me: "Could you lend me some money? I want to go in." I agree to. (She looked like Betzi, but no, it wasn't her.) I give her the money, she pays, and then turns her back on me. "How rude!" I think. Eventually, I stop concerning myself about it. Then I too go in without even looking at her. Later, I unintentionally discover her buying a box of popcorn. I wait. I see that she quietly enters the auditorium and looks for an orchestra seat. Indiscreetly, I follow her and sit down next to her. Good, perfect move, Messeguer. Out of the corner of my eye I look at her tremendous breasts, her slender body. As soon as the film begins the lights go out. I try to concentrate. But I can't. I keep my attention on her. I feel uncomfortable, embarrassed. More out of an obligation to instinct than to conscience, I put my hand on her knee. She wears nylon stockings that make her thin legs smooth. I wait. I know that from one moment to the next she would slap me. My hand is stiff. Sweaty. God, the slap doesn't arrive. What joy! But the hand starts to sweat. I see myself forced to remove it and pull a handkerchief out of my pocket to dry it. Flirting, in the meantime, she tidies up her dress and erotically pulls on the strap of her bra. I'm aroused. I suppose that she too felt desire. Quickly I remember that I'm married to Betzi. Shit! Once again I place my hand on her knee and I let it slide. Fascinated, nervous, she lifts her buttock upwards and gets comfortable. She's asking me for more . . . I know it. And I'll give her more. I gently bring my hand up to her thighs and oh, what a surprise!, I realize that underneath her slip, amongst those very confused, protective ligaments . . . she wasn't wearing any underwear. I started breathing faster.

The bald headed man sitting in the orchestra seat in front of us suspected something. He knows that we're not watching the film. He turns around to make sure that everything is all right. No. He turns around because he's jealous of me. He wants to snatch *my* woman away from me. I place my hand across my face because I don't want him to see me. She's probably his wife, I think. No, if she was his wife they would be sitting next to each other. I place my hand on her knee again and quickly find her private part. I find that savage jungle that fills me with passion. I become insane. I try to trap her. Meanwhile, she acts as if nothing was happening, not even batting an eyelid. Hey, this frolicking is nice! I keep fondling her. I should suggest that we go to a hotel or ask her out to dinner. I remove my hand and I quickly discover . . . oh, no! . . . I discover that once again I've lost my ring. Impossible, it's a trick. I'm an idiot. "Lady, I lost my ring," I tell her. She doesn't react. I return to the scene of passion. I introduce my hand again, and then bend down to look. Nothing, not a trace of the damned ring. I insert one of my hands completely, then the other hand. It's a very large, deep, and bottomless hole—a wintry cave. I look up and she's still watching Marlene Dietrich. Shit! What a mess I've gotten myself into. Determined, I bend down once more. Both of my hands and then my head go inside. I'm afraid the bald-headed man could report me. Quiet, Messeguer, do it carefully. I insert my feet and then my entire body. I completely enter that abyss, and it is totally dark. I light a match. It's impossible that the ring could have vanished. I illuminate the area from one side to the other with the lit match. Nothing. My God! I have the feeling that the medusa is going to appear soon. I start walking. I walk. I hear deep voices in the distance. Perhaps they're sounds coming from the film. A jelly-like liquid, having dripped onto the floor, makes it difficult for me to walk. My breathing is awkward. And what if I wanted to return? Yes, I want to return. I want to return but I'm lost. I've lost myself. I scream. I tell myself: Scream Messeguer, louder . . . louder. "Give me back my ring." I hope that the bald headed man can come to save me. Nothing. My hands are sweating. Suddenly I see a couple. I get closer and discover that it's . . . Betzi—accompanied by some stranger. Sure, her deception was obvious. My brother was right. I hear her say something about Rochester even though I can barely decipher the syllables. I soon discover that the stranger standing beside her is wearing my ring on the pinky finger of his left hand. Betzi then says something more about the trip. Yes, they should know the way back perfectly. Would it be indiscreet to ask them to return my ring? "Hey, friend," I tell him slyly, "you're wearing my ring." I look at his face. It's impossible . . . the person who is accompanying Betzi is me.

That was the last time we saw each other.

⁕━━━━⁕

TRANSLATED BY HARRY MORALES

My heart is in the East and I am at the edge of the West. Then how can I taste what I eat, how can I enjoy it? How can I fulfill my vows and pledges while Zion is in the domain of Edom, and I am in the bonds of Arabia?

JUDAH HALEVI

Work of good prose has three steps: a musical stage when it is composed, an architectonic one when it is built, and a textile one when it is woven.

WALTER BENJAMIN

I WAS BORN IN MEXICO CITY, 7 APRIL 1961, ON A CLOUDY DAY WITHOUT major historical events. I am a descendant of Jews from Russia and Poland, businessmen and rabbis, that arrived by sheer chance in Veracruz, on the Atlantic coast next to the Yucatán peninsula. I am a sum of parts and thus lace purity of blood (what proud renaissance Iberians called *la pureza de sangre*): white Caucasian with a Mediterranean twist, much like the Enlightenment philosopher Moses Mendelssohn and only marginally like the Aztec poet Ollin Yollistli. My idols, not surprisingly, are Spinoza and Kafka, two exiles in their own land who chose unmaternal languages (Portuguese and Hebrew to Latin, Czech to German) in order to elevate themselves to a higher order, and who, relentlessly, investigated their own spirituality beyond the realm of orthodox religion and routine. Ralph Waldo Emerson, in *Essays: Second Series* (1844), says that the reason we feel one man's presence and not another's is as simple as gravity. I have traveled from Spanish into Yiddish, Hebrew, and English; from my native home south of the Rio Grande far and away—to Europe, the Middle East, the United States, the Bahamas, and South America—always in search of the ultimate clue to the mysteries of my divided identity. What I found is doubt.

I grew up in an intellectually sophisticated middle-class, in a secure, self-imposed Jewish ghetto (a treasure island) where gentiles hardly existed. Money and comfort, books, theater and art. Since early on I was sent to Yiddish day school, Colegio Israelita de México in Colonia Narvarte, where the heroes were Sholom Aleichem and Theodor Herzl while people like José Joaquín Fernández de Lizardi, Agustín Yáñez, Juan Rulfo, and Octavio Paz were almost unknown; that is, we lived in an oasis completely uninvolved with things Mexican. In fact, when it came to knowledge of the outside world, students were far better off talking about U.S. products (Hollywood, TV, junk food, technology) than about matters native—an artificial capsule, our ghetto, much like the magical sphere imagined by Blaise Pascal: its diameter everywhere and its center nowhere.

Mother tongue. The expression crashed into my mind at age twenty, perhaps a bit later. The father tongue, I assumed, was the adopted alternative and illegitimate language (Henry James preferred the term "wife tongue"), whereas the mother tongue is genuine and authentic—a uterus: the original source. I was educated in (into) four idioms: Spanish, Yiddish, Hebrew, and English. Spanish was the public venue; Hebrew was a channel toward Zionism and not toward the sacredness of the synagogue; Yiddish symbolized the Holocaust and past struggles of the Eastern European labor movement; and English was the entrance door to redemption: the United States. Abba Eban said it better: Jews are like everybody else . . . except a little bit more. A polyglot, of course, has as many loyalties as homes. Spanish is my right eye, English my left; Yiddish my background and Hebrew my conscience. Or better, each of the four represents a different set of spectacles (near-sight, bifocal, night-reading, etc.) through which the universe is seen.

THE ABUNDANCE OF SELF

This multifarious (is there such a word?) upbringing often brought me difficulties. Around the neighborhood, I was always *el güerito* and *el ruso*. Annoyingly, my complete name is Ilan Stavchansky Slomianski; nobody, except for Yiddish teachers, knew how to pronounce it. (I get mail addressed to Ivan Starlominsky, Isvan Estafchansky, and Allen Stevens.) After graduating from high school, most of my friends, members of richer families, were sent abroad, to the U.S. or Israel, to study. Those that remained, including me, were forced to go to college at home to face Mexico *tête a tête*. The shock was tremendous. Suddenly, I (we) recognized the artificiality of our oasis. What to do? I, for one, rejected my background. I felt Judaism made me a pariah. I wanted to be an authentic Mexican and thus foolishly joined the Communist cause but the result wasn't pleasing. Among the *camaradas*, I was also "the blondy" and "the Jew." No hope, no escape. So I decided to investigate my ethnic and religious past obsessively and made it my duty to fully understand guys like Maimonides, Arthur Koestler, Mendelssohn, Judah Halevi, Hasdai Crescas, Spinoza, Walter Benjamin, Gershom Scholem, Martin Buber, Franz Rosenzweig, Abraham Joshua Heschel. . . . It helped, at least temporarily—nothing lasts forever.

Years later, while teaching medieval philosophy at Universidad Iberoamericana, a Jesuit college in downtown Mexico City, during the 1982 Lebanon invasion, a group of Palestinian sympathizers threw rotten tomatoes at me and my students (99 percent gentiles). Eager to manifest their anger and protest, they had to find an easy target and I was the closest link to Israel around. The whole thing reminded me of a scene that took place at age fourteen, while sitting in Yiddish class at Colegio Israelita. Mr. Lockier, the teacher, was reading from I. J. Singer's *The Family Carnovsky*—the story of three generations in a German-Jewish family enchanted with the nineteenth-century Enlightenment, slowly but surely becoming assimilated into German society until the tragic uprise of Nazism brought unthinkable consequences. The monotonous rhythm of the recitations was boring and nobody was paying much attention. Suddenly, a segment of the story truly captivated me: the moment when Jegor, eldest son of Dr. David Carnov-sky's mixed marriage to Teresa Holbeck, is ridiculed in class by Professor Kirch-enmeier, a newly appointed principal at the Goethe Gymnasium in Berlin. Singer describes the event meticulously: Nazism is on the rise: the aristocracy, and more specifically the Jews, are anxious to know the overall outcome of the violent acts taking place daily on the city street. Racial theories are being discussed and Aryans glorified. Feverishly anti-Jewish, Kirchenmeier, while delivering a lecture, calls Jegor to the front to use him as a guinea pig in illustrating his theories. With compass and calipers, he measures the length and width of the boy's skull, writing the figures on the board. He then measures the distance from ear to ear, from the top of the head to the chin, and the length of the nose. A packed auditorium is silently watching. Jegor is then asked to undress. He is terrified and hesitates, of course; he is ashamed and feels conspicuous because of his circumcision. Eventually other students, persuaded by Kirchenmeier, help undress the Jew, and the teacher proceeds to show in the "inferior" Jewish strain the marks of the rib structure. He finishes by calling attention to Jegor's geni-talia, whose premature development shows "the degenerate sexuality of the Semitic race."

Astonishment. What troubled me most was Jegor's inaction. I suppose it was natural to be petrified in such a situation, but I refused to justify his immobility. So I interrupted Mr. Lockier to ask why didn't the boy es-cape. A deadly silence invaded the classroom. It was clear I had disturbed the other students' sleep and the teacher's rhythm. "Because . . . he couldn't. He simply couldn't," was the answer I got. "Because that's the way lives are written. . . ." I don't know or care what happened next. As years went by I came to understand that concept, the almighty Author of Authors, as intriguing, and the scene in Yiddish class as an allegory of myself and Mexican Jews as an easy and palatable target of animosity. At the Jesuit college almost a decade later, I was the marionette-holder's Jegor Carnovsky—God's joy and toy: the Jew.

KALEIDOSCOPE

Bizarre combination—Mexican Jews: some 60,000 frontier dwellers and hyphen people like Dr. Jekyll and Mr. Hyde, a sum of sums of parts, a multiplicity of multiplicities. Although settlers from Germany began to arrive in "Aztec Country" around 1830, the very first synagogue was not built in the nation's capital until some fifty-five years later. From then on, waves of Jewish immigrants came from Russia and Central and Eastern Europe, Ashkenazim whose goal was to make it big in New York (the Golden Land) but since an immigration quota was imposed in the United States in 1921, a little detour places them in Cuba, Puerto Rico, or the Gulf of Mexico (the Rotten Land). Most were Yiddish-speaking Bundists: hard-working peasants, businessmen, and teachers, nonreligious and entrepreneurial, escaping Church-sponsored pogroms and government persecution whose primary dream was never Palestine. Hardly anything physical or ideological differentiated them from the relatives that did make it north, to Chicago, Detroit, Pittsburgh, and the Lower East Side—except, of course, the fact that they, disoriented immigrants, couldn't settle where they pleased. And this sense of displacement colored our future.

Migration and its discontent. I have often imagined the culture shock, surely not too drastic, my forefathers experienced at their arrival: from *mujik* to *campesino*, similar types in a different milieu. Mexico was packed with colonial monasteries where fanatical nuns prayed day and night. Around 1910 Emiliano Zapata and Pancho Villa were making their Socialist Revolution, and an anti-Church feeling (known in Mexico as *La Cristiada* and master-fully examined in Graham Greene's *The Power and the Glory*) was rampant. Aztecs, the legend claimed, once sacrificed daughters to their idols in sky-high pyramids and perhaps were cannibals. Undoubtedly this was to be a transitory stop, it had to. It was humid and at least in the nation's capital, nature remained in an eternal autumn.

I must confess never to have learned to love Mexico. I was taught to re-tain a sense of foreignness—as a tourist without a home. The best literature I know about Mexico is by Europeans and U.S. writers: Italo Calvino, André Breton, Jack Kerouac, Graham Greene, Joseph Brodsky, Antonin Artaud, Katherine Anne Porter, Malcolm Lowry, Harriet Doerr . . . I only love my country when I am far and away. Elsewhere—that's where I belong: the vast diaspora. Nowhere and everywhere. (Am I a name dropper? Me, whose name no one can pronounce?)

OUT OF THE BASEMENT

When the Mexican edition of *Talia in Heaven* (1989) came out, my pub-lisher, Fernando Valdés, at a reception, talked about the merits of this, my first (and so far only) novel. He applauded this and that ingredient, spoke highly of the innovative style, and congratulated the author for his pre-cocious artistic maturity. Memory has deleted most of his comments. I no longer remember what he liked and why. The only sentence that still ticks in my mind, the one capable of overcoming the passing of time, came at the end of his speech, when he said: "For many centuries, Latin America has had Jews living in its basement, great writers creating out of the shadow. And Ilan Stavans is the one I kept hidden until now." A frighten-ing metaphor.

In the past five hundred years, Jews in the Hispanic world have been forced to convert to Christianity or somehow to mask or feel ashamed of their ancestral faith. Their intellectual contribution, notwithstanding, has been enormous. Spanish letters cannot be understood without Fray Luis de León and Ludovicus Vives, without Fernando de Roja's *La Celestina* and the anti-Semitic poetry of Francisco de Quevedo, author of the infamous sonnet "A man stuck to a nose." *(Erase un hombre a una nariz pegado, érase una nariz superlativa, érase una alquitara medio viva, érase un peje espada mal barbado . . .)* In the Americas, a safe haven for refugees from the Inquisition and later on for Eastern Europeans running away from the Nazis, Jewish writers have been active since 1910, when Alberto Gerchunoff, a Russian immigrant, published in Spanish his collection of interrelated vignettes, *The Jewish Gauchos of La Pampa*, to commemorate Argentina's independence. He switched from one language to another to seek individual freedom, to validate his democratic spirit, to embrace a dream of plurality and progress: Yiddish, the tongue of Mendel Mokher Sforim and Sholem Aleichem, was left behind; Spanish, Cervantes' vehicle of communication—Gerchunoff was an admirer of *Don Quixote*—became the new tool, the channel to entertain, educate, and redeem the masses. Like Spinoza, Kafka, Nabokov, and Joseph Brodsky, he was the ultimate translator: a bridge between idiosyncrasies.

The abyss and the bridge. Many decades later, some fifty astonishing writers from Buenos Aires and Mexico to Lima and Guatemala, including Moacyr Scliar, Clarice Lispector, and Mario Szichman, continue to carry of Gerchunoff's torch . . . but the world knows little about them. The narrative boom that catapulted Gabriel García Márquez, Carlos Fuentes, and others from south of the Rio Grande to international stardom in the sixties managed to sell a monolithic, suffocatingly uniform image of the entire continent as a Banana Republic crowded with clairvoyant prostitutes and forgotten generals, never a multicultural society. To such a degree were ethnic voices left in the margin that readers today know much more about Brazilian and Argentine Jews thanks to Borges' short stories "Emma Zunz" and "The Secret Miracle," and Vargas Llosa's novel *The Storyteller*, than to anything written by Gerchunoff and his followers. Sadly and in spite of his anti-Semitic tone, my Mexican publisher was right: in the baroque architecture of Latin American letters, Jews inhabit the basement. And yet, *la pureza de sangre* in the Hispanic world is but an abstraction: native Indians, Jews, Arabs, Africans, Christians . . . the collective identity is always in need of a hyphen. In spite of the "official" image stubbornly promoted by governments from time immemorial, Octavio Paz and Julio Cortázar have convincingly used the salamander, the *axólotl*, as a symbol to describe Latin America's popular soul, always ambiguous and in mutation.

AMERICA, AMERICA

I honestly never imagined I could one day pick up my suitcases to leave home once and for all. And yet, at twenty-five I moved to New York. I was awarded a scholarship to study for a master's at the Jewish Theological Seminary and, afterwards, perhaps a doctorate at Columbia University or elsewhere. I fled Mexico (and Spanish) mainly because as a secular Jew—what Freud would have called "a psychological Jew"—I felt marginalized, a stereotypes. (Little did I know!) A true chameleon, a bit parochial and near-sighted, a nonconformist with big dreams and few possibilities. Like my globe-trotting Hebraic ancestors, I had been raised to build an ivory tower, an individual ghetto. By choosing to leave, I turned my past into remembrance: I left the basement and ceased to be a pariah. *Talia in Heaven* exemplifies that existential dilemma: its message simultaneously encourages Jews to integrate and openly invites them to escape; it alternates between life and memory. Paraphrasing Lionel Trilling, its cast of characters, victims of an obsessive God (much like the Bible's) who enjoys ridiculing them, are at the bloody crossroad where politics, theology, and literature meet.

To be or not: To be. The moment I crossed the border, I became somebody else: a new person. In *Chromos: A Parody of Truth*, Felipe Alfau says: "The moment one learns English, complications set in. Try as one may, one cannot elude this conclusion, one must inevitably come back to it." While hoping to master the English language during sleepless nights, I understood James Baldwin, who, already exiled in Paris and quoting Henry James, claimed it is a complex fate to be an American. "America's history," the black author of *Nobody Knows My Name* wrote, "her aspirations, her peculiar triumphs, her even more peculiar defeats, and her position in the world—yesterday and today—are all so profoundly and stubbornly unique that the very word "America" remains a new, almost completely undefined and extremely controversial proper noun. No one in the world seems to know exactly what it describes." To be honest, the rise of multiculturalism, which perceives the melting pot as a soup of diverse and at times incompatible backgrounds, has made the word "America" even more troublesome, more evasive and abstract: Is America a compact whole, a unity? Is it a sum of ethnic groups unified by a single language and a handful of patriotic symbols? Is it a Quixotic dream where total assimilation is impossible, where multiculturalism is to lead to disintegration? And Baldwin's statement acquires a totally different connotation when one goes one step beyond, realizing that "America" is not only a nation (a state of mind) but also a vast continent. From Alaska to the Argentine pampa, from Rio de Janeiro to East Los Angeles, the geography Christopher Columbus mistakenly encountered in 1492 and Amerigo Vespucci baptized a few years later is also a linguistic and cultural addition: America the nation and America the continent. America, America: I wanted to find a room of my own in the two; or two rooms, perhaps?

On Being a White Hispanic and More

Once settled, I suddenly began to be perceived as Hispanic (i.e., Latino)—an identity totally alien to me before. (My knowledge of spoken Latin is minimal.) To make matters worse, my name (once again?), accent, and skin color were exceptions to what gringos had as "the Hispanic prototype." In other words, in Mexico I was perceived as Jewish; and now across the border, I was Mexican. Funny, isn't it? (I face, according to official papers I qualify as a white Hispanic, an unpleasant term if there was ever one.) Once again, an impostor, an echo. (An impostor, says Ambrose Bierce in *The Devil's Dictionary*, is a rival aspirant to public honors.)

Themselves, myself. Hispanics in the United States—some 22,254,059 according to the 1990 census: white, black, yellow, green, blue, red . . . , twice Americans, once in spite of themselves. They have been in the territories north of the Rio Grande even before the Pilgrims of the Mayflower; and with the Guadalupe Hidalgo Treaty signed in 1848, in which Generalísimo Antonio López de Santa Ana gave away and subsequently sold half of Mexico to the White House (why only half?), many of them unexpectedly, even unwillingly, became a part of an Anglo-Saxon, English-speaking reality. Today, after decades of neglect and silence, decades of anonymity and ignorance, Latinos are finally receiving the attention they deserve. The second fastest-growing ethnic group after the Asians, their diversity of roots—Caribbean, Mexican, Central and South American, Iberian, and so on—makes them a difficult collectivity to describe. Are the Cuban migrations from Holguín, Matanzas, and Havana similar in their idiosyncratic attitude to that of Managua, San Salvador, and Santo Domingo? Is the Spanish they speak their true *lingua franca*, the only unifying factor? Is their immigrant experience in any way different from that of previous minorities—Irish, Italian, Jewish, what have you? How do they understand and assimilate the complexities of what it means to be American? And where do I, a white Hispanic, fit in?

Nowhere and everywhere. In 1985 I was assigned by a Spanish magazine to interview Isaac Goldemberg, a famous Jewish-Peruvian novelist who wrote *The Fragmented Life of Don Jacobo Lerner*. When we met at the Hungarian Pastry Shop at Amsterdam Avenue and 110th Street, he told me, among many things, he had been living in New York for over two decades without mastering the English language because he didn't want his Spanish to suffer and ultimately evaporate. Borges says in his short story "The Life of Tadeo Isidoro Cruz (1829–1874)": "Any life, no matter how long or complex it may be, is made up essentially of a *single moment*—the moment in which a man finds out, once and for all, who he is." That summer day I understood my linguistic future lay in the opposite direction from Goldemberg's: I would perfect my English and thus become a New York Jew, an intellectual animal in the proud tradition celebrated by Alfred Kazin . . . and I did. In just a single moment I understood who I could be.

THE DOUBLE

To write is to make sense of confusion in and around. Didn't somebody already say this? Jean Genet, John Updike? I am a copy, an instant replay, a shadow, an impostor. Everything is an echo. To live is to plagiarize, to imitate, to steal.

I have always had the feeling of living somebody else's life. When I first read Felipe Alfau's *Locos: A Comedy of Gestures*, I was possessed by the idea that, had I been born in 1902 in Barcelona, as had its author, I would have written his book. The exact same sensation was repeated when discovering Pinhas "Der Nister" Kahanovitch's *The Family Mashber*, a masterpiece of Soviet Jewish fiction by a writer who died in a Russian hospital in 1950 as a result of Stalin's purges. And my mother keeps a yellowish school photograph I once gave her. It was taken when I was eight or nine: although smiling, I really don't look happy; and in the back it has a brief line written: "With love from a non-existent twin brother." Furthermore, I am often sure I am being observed by an omniscient Creature (with capital "C"), who enjoys inflicting pain and laughs at the sorrow of His creatures. I cannot but equate the act of writing to God's impact on Nature: He is simultaneously absent and present in His creation, granting birth and death—the Absolute Novelist, a marionette-holder with a vivid imagination and a bad sense of humor (even if He laughs).

"Total Forgetery"

Acting—my father's trade.

As I was growing up, I remember feeling amazed by his incredible talent. I adored him. Watching his performances, I would be pushed to what Sören Kierkegaard regarded as "an existential vacuum—a mystery." Was he really the man I knew or, instead, a mask-carrier? I was particularly fond of him taking me along on Sunday afternoons. We would leave home alone after lunch. While driving an old Rambler, he would ask me about school and friends, about ideas and books, masturbation and a girl's sexuality. He was a hero, a man of integrity like few others, the only guy I knew who was actually happy, very happy, a few minutes every day: on stage. Then, as my father would park the car, I would begin noticing a slow change of attitude, a metamorphosis, as if a veil, an abyss was now setting us apart. Another self would graciously descend to possess him, to take the man I knew and loved away from me. A few minutes later, I would witness how, without shame, he would undress in front of a mirror, put on a bathrobe, and begin to hide his face in cosmetics. He was becoming somebody else, a stranger, a ghost: today a hotel owner, next season a boxer, a cancer patient, a Jewish prisoner in Germany. His breathtaking masks were infallible: they always hid my dad's true self, deformed it. As a result of that transformation, I felt totally alone.

Alone and lonely. The whole phenomenon inspired in me mixed feelings: I was astonished by the magic and frightened at the same time; I hated the whole thing and yet would literally do anything to return tomorrow and witness it anew. My father would then ask a handyman to seat me behind the stage, next to a curtain, in order for me to watch the show. And that, oh God, was his and my greatest moment on earth, the one we awaited even more eagerly than the facial and physical change he underwent to become a character. With a difference: In front of an audience, he was happy; I, on the other hand, was scared to death—invaded by the kind of fear that simultaneously generates joy and sorrow. What did others think of his "new" self? Could they recognize the true face behind the mask? Was he an impostor?

Alone and lonely and full of envy. I would feel an overwhelming sense of envy, profound and disturbing jealousy toward the audience. They received all his attention, which, in normal circumstances, I would keep for my own, or at most, share with my brother and sister. They would be manipulated, seduced by his talents. Why was he so eager to become other people and take a rest from himself? And hide behind a mask? Even more suspiciously, why did the viewers pay to have him taken away from me? How could people pay for my father to cease being himself? The Author of Authors, the Impostor of Impostors: God as playwright. In my eyes, the entire universe was a vast and mysterious theater in which he (Yahweh, Adonai, Elohim, the Holy Spirit, the Father of Fathers) would capriciously establish what people, the actors, are to do, to say, to think, to hope. My dad's actual stage was a microcosmos that inspired me to philosophize about religion and eschatology, about freedom and determinism. I wondered: while acting, was my father free to refuse pronouncing a certain line of the script?; could he talk to me at least once during the performance (through his real and unimported self)? I also wondered if I, Ilan Stavans (aka, Ilan Stavchansky Slomianski), was free to stop being his son?; could I also become other people—like Shakespeare, be one and many? To answer these many questions, I became a novelist. To write is to make sense of confusion in and around. (It was me who said that.)

To write, perchance to dream. (Or vice versa?) Not long ago an interviewer asked me why didn't I follow his footsteps and enter the stage. My response was short and somewhat condescending. Deep inside, I dislike actors. I find their vulnerability, their trendiness and exhibitionism disturbing. I would rather live in the shadow than in the spotlight. Besides, I love the theater of the mind and have a terrible fear of dying. It might sound absurd but I see literature as brother to memory and theater as a symbol of the ephemeral present. I write in order to remember and be remembered. Death is the absence of recollection—what Luis G. Rodriguez calls "total forgetery." Theater, on the other hand, is a *performance* art, a transitory game. It is only alive during a night show, afterwards it's gone . . . forever. Nothing remains, nothing. Except perhaps a handful of yellowish photos and (luck permitting) an award or two. And if theater is like a vanishing photograph, writing is signing one's name on concrete: a proof of existence ("I was here . . ."). By incorporating past and present images, a narrative plays with Time (with a capital "T") in an astonishing fashion: it makes reality eternal. Marcel's desire for his mother's goodnight kiss in Proust's *Remembrance of Things Past* is not a pre–World War I scene alone but, unquestionably, an image for the ages. When death turns me into a ghost, at least something, an ingenious thought or a breath of life, will remain—a written page like those of Virgil, Dante, and Cervantes. Perhaps and perhaps not. The only certainty is that a library is a triumph over nothingness. And yet, the warm human contact my dad encounters while performing is always reinvigorating. Literature, on the other hand, is a secluded activity. Isolation, silence, detachment, escape. You hope someone will read you someday, although nothing (not even the timing of God's laughter) is certain. Thus, decades away of those Sunday afternoons when my father would take me along to his show, I still confess I feel envy: He can be happy, I cannot. I honestly wish I could at times take vacations from myself—like him, have another self. It must be refreshing. Isolation, silence.

Before death and after. Literature, I am perfectly aware, is no palliative to cure a spirit's suffering. The day I die, people will not interrupt their routines, why should they? They will make love, eat, defecate, smoke, and read. They will smile and cry and kiss and hate. It will matter to no one (not even my dearest ones, really) that my life has ceased to be and all is over. The show will go on. Grief—a strange and dishonest feeling. When Calvino and Danilos Kiš, two mentors, died, did I cry? (Albert Camus' protagonist in

The Stranger is incarcerated for not crying during his mother's funeral.) I did pray for their souls and after that . . . after that, nothing. Only through literature, I feel, can I transcend myself. To write is to overcome the imperfections of nature. I do it every day, every day, every day, every . . . ; otherwise, I sense that a day's 86,400 seconds are meaningless and in vain.

THINGS TO COME

A future encyclopaedia, to be published in Brussels in 2087, states that at age thirty-one I wrote a book, *Imagining Columbus*, about the Genoese admiral's fifth and final voyage of discovery, one not across the Atlantic but through the human imagination. That I was the author of a controversial reflection on the identity of Hispanics in the United States, and a volume of early short stories, collectively called in English *The One-Handed Pianist*. It mentions the fact that somewhere after 1995, I published a novel about a Belgian actor of Jewish descent, who has trouble distinguishing where reality ends and fantasy begins (poor Konstantin Stanislavski! Or is it Konstantin Stavchansky?)—inspired, obviously, by my dad's trade; translated into numerous languages, the volume was enthusiastically received by critics and readers. Afterwards, I wrote another novel, this one in the style of Vargas Llosa, about the exiled family of a Latin American dictator, after which I won numerous grants and prizes, was internationally applauded and commemorated.

It discusses my multilingualism. After a literary beginning as a Yiddish playwright and short fiction writer, I moved first into Spanish and then into English, translating and reinventing myself. (Although I wrote English with ease and distinction, I spoke like a tourist). If, as Nabokov once claimed, our existence is but a brief crack of light between two eternities of darkness, why not take advantage and be two writers at once? The entry also states that I left an echo, an echo, an echo. Critics prized my oeuvre, comparing it to precursors and successors like Kafka, Spinoza, and Borges. Because of my dual identity, in Mexico I was considered a "bad citizen." My themes always dealt with God as manipulator of human conscience and my existential journey could be reduced to a verse by the Nicaraguan *modernista* poet Rubén Darío: "To be and not to know. . . ." My style was precise and direct, akin to religious insights. Cyril Connolly says in *Unquiet Grave:* "The more books we read, the sooner we perceive that the only function of a writer is to produce a masterpiece. No other task is of any consequence." The encyclopaedia claims that toward the end of life, I wrote extraordinarily lasting short stories, as if everything that preceded them was a prophecy. Finally, it states that I died on 18 August 2033, with some twenty-two original books to my credit. After a consuming sickness, I contemplated suicide but a sudden heart attack impeded me from arriving at a nearby New York hospital and nothingness took over. That was also a rainy day without major historical events. God witnessed my death and pretended to suffer, although His was of course an actor's gesture. In fact, He laughed: I was (am) His joy and toy.